claire mackay
MINI~BIKE RESCUE

Cover by Mike McKeever

Scholastic-TAB Publications Ltd.
123 Newkirk Road, Richmond Hill, Ontario, Canada

The author acknowledges use of the following passages:

"Trouble in Mind" words and music by Richard
M. Jones
© copyright 1926, 1937 by MCA Music Canada, a
division of MCA Canada Ltd., Toronto, Ontario.
Copyright renewed.
Used by permission. All rights reserved.

page 38, from "On First Looking Into Chapman's Homer"
by John Keats
page 59, from *Walden* by Henry David Thoreau

ISBN 0-590-71100-8

Published by Scholastic-TAB Publications Ltd.,
123 Newkirk Road, Richmond Hill, Ontario, Canada L4C 3G5

3rd printing 1985   Printed in Canada

To Will Elder,
who kept me on a straight track

Other books by Claire Mackay

Mini-Bike Hero

Mini-Bike Racer

Exit Barney McGee

Contents

1 No more biking 1

2 A first-class villain 10

3 The dead place 21

4 Let's go, Champ! 29

5 Don't look down! 36

6 Probably harmless 46

7 Alias Prince Charming 54

8 Dear Julie 63

9 You talk too much! 72

10 Purdy and Craven Enterprises 84

11 Out of the frying pan 97

12 Another lie 108

13 It's no use! 118

14 A different drummer 127

Trouble in mind, I'm blue,
But I won't be blue always
'Cause the sun gonna shine
In my back door some day.

I'm gonna lay my head
On some lonesome railroad line
And let the two-nineteen
Pacify my mind.

Well, trouble, oh trouble,
Trouble on my worried mind;
When you see me laughin'
It's just to keep from cryin'.

1

No more biking

"You *what?*"

"I threw it out."

Julie's mouth fell open in disbelief, then closed with a snap, her jaw square and angry below narrowed green eyes. She slammed her bedroom door and hurtled downstairs, taking the last three steps as one, to face her mother in the big farm kitchen.

"You threw out my mini-biking sweater?"

"I threw out the old blue sweater with the huge hole in the elbow and the ravelled edges, if that's what you mean," said Mrs. Brennan, calmly peeling carrots.

"But Mom, you know I wear it mini-biking all the time. It's my lucky sweater, the one I wore when I won the race last year! How come you threw it out? And why do you muck around with my stuff anyway?"

Mrs. Brennan went on peeling carrots, slowly,

methodically, one by one. When Julie ran out of breath she said, "You shouldn't yell, Julie. It's not ladylike."

"Ladylike?" yelled Julie. "What's that got to do with anything? Especially my sweater?"

Her mother put the carrots in a pot and put the pot on the stove. Then she turned, wiping her hands on her apron. "It's more important than you seem to think, Julie." A frown crossed her face as she looked at her daughter, at the patched jeans and the dirty Adidas, at the T-shirt Steve MacPherson had given her, with *BIG MAMA BIKER* splashed across the front in purple Day-Glo letters. "You're thirteen now. You've got to think about growing up, about—about doing things other girls do."

"Like what?" It sounded rude, Julie knew, but she couldn't stop herself. She felt reckless with anger.

"Like your clothes, for one thing," said her mother, and her voice had an edge Julie recognized. She knew what was coming, could almost recite it by heart. For a moment she was tempted. Except it would freak her mother right out. So she pretended to listen to the long and utterly boring lecture on what a mess she was, what a mess her bedroom was, why did she have to wear that shirt, and why couldn't she be more like Roxanna Peters over on the next farm. Who was perfect. In everything. Who never yelled, whose bedroom was neat as a jail cell, who already knew how to make chili sauce, and who spent her time embroidering pillow cases for when she got married. Julie snorted.

Her mother's voice intruded. "And what's more, I really don't want you riding all over the countryside with that Steve and his friend, whatever his name is."

Julie felt a cold stillness forming inside her. Her hands dropped from her hips and curled into fists. She had a prickling sense of danger, a feeling that other words—ugly, hurting words—were hiding behind those her mother had spoken.

She forced herself to speak carefully. "Steve's friend is named Kim, Mom. And what exactly do you mean by 'that Steve'? I always thought you and Dad liked him okay."

Her mother's glance slid away. "Well, yes, of course we do, but..." She investigated the pot of carrots as if it could finish her sentence. Julie watched her and waited.

Mrs. Brennan turned at last. Her face was flushed, her voice loud as she said, "Really, Julie, I don't want you to spend so much time with him. People are starting to talk about it. And about the mini-biking too. It was all right when you were younger, but now you should have other interests. And other friends. It's not—not healthy!"

Julie gripped the kitchen chair in front of her and her voice trembled only a little when she asked, "What are people saying, Mom? And what people? Mrs. Peters, for example? Or Roxanna? She always was a meanmouth!" In spite of herself her voice rose. "And what do *you* think, Mom? You think Steve and I might ride off into the sunset and elope one night? What a bunch of—" Julie closed her mouth abruptly. If she said the word she'd been thinking her mom would really have a fit. A ladylike one, of course.

Her mother turned back to the stove. Oh terrific, Julie thought. Now she doesn't even want to look at me. Boy, am I that bad? All of a sudden she felt more hurt than angry. She could feel a lump in her throat and swallowed it down. No kid's trick right now. This was too important. And then her mother said something really unbelievable.

"Well, Julie, it's not something we'll be arguing about much longer, since you're going away for the summer."

"I'm going away for the summer?" Julie yelled.

"Yes. To Aunt Maureen's in Ontario. I talked to her last night. What with Uncle Tim gone, she needs help to run the snack bar and keep the cabins clean. I told her you'd be glad to come. It'll be a nice change for you, instead of hanging around here for months."

All the sentences came out in a jerky way, without proper breaths between them. As if her mother had rehearsed them, Julie thought.

She exploded. "But Mom, I had my summer all planned! The big race is next October and Steve and I were all set to practise like mad. We've already laid out a course and everything. How could you do this? You didn't even ask me! Don't I have a say in my own life? Do I just get ordered around like a slave? I don't want to go! I won't go! That's all there is to it! Aunt Mo will just have to get a maid someplace else. It's not my fault Uncle Tim died last winter. I can't go and I won't go!"

Her mother swung round and faced her, her mouth set in the same grim lines as her daughter's. "I'm sorry, Julie. It's all settled. You're going. You leave on the Saturday morning plane."

Julie stared at her mother, the rage and hurt plain in her white face. Mrs. Brennan flinched, then took a step forward, her hand raised as if in apology.

"Don't you come near me, Mom! I'll never forgive you for this!" Julie wheeled, grabbed her jean jacket off the hook at the back door and ran from the house.

A moment later the afternoon echoed with the roar of the little Mohawk as it sped up the trail to the ridge.

*   *   *

Julie hadn't looked back, even though at the last minute, just before she'd walked through the glass doors onto the tarmac, she had wanted so much to turn around, to wave to her mother, to look at her face and know that things were all right again. They had hardly spoken since the fight. And her father had been no help: he'd stayed out in the fields most of the day, and at mealtimes, when he couldn't avoid noticing the silence, all he did was grunt and look uncomfortable.

When her mother had bent to kiss her, Julie had kept her face tight and still, had made no move to kiss her back. She had said goodbye as if her mother were a stranger, and had walked away. No, she hadn't looked back.

But now, as the plane taxied, as the enormous engines thundered beside her, as they gathered speed on the runway, Julie looked out the window at the little terminal, hoping for one last glimpse. Then, with a sudden lift, a sudden sharper tone in the engines, the aircraft rose from the ground and began its long ascent.

Turning in her seat, Julie peered down at Murdoch Corners. She tried to find the big half-section farm that was her home, and the ridge of tall poplars where she and Steve rode their bikes. But they had already disappeared. As the plane began to level out, she felt very small and very lonely.

Maybe she was wrong, she thought. Maybe she should give in. Her mother had been right about lots of things before. Maybe she should be different, more like Roxanna. At that thought her mouth tightened. No way! Absolutely no way! Even if everybody in the whole world thought she was weird, she sure as heck wasn't going to be like Roxanna!

Besides, Julie had to admit she was sort of excited. The summer might even turn out to be an adventure. With one big bonus: her mother wouldn't be yakking at her all the time. She'd be on her own. No parents, no brother, no sister. Just old Aunt Mo—who'd be far too busy to be a watchdog. Hey, hey! Things might be okay after all!

She sat up straighter in her seat and casually unlatched the seatbelt, like the man sitting next to her. The attendant stopped in the aisle beside them.

"Would you like something to drink?"

Julie looked at her blankly for a moment, then said, deadpan, as a line of dialogue from an old movie came to her, "Yes, I'll have a dry martini, please. Better make it a double."

The attendant laughed. So did the man beside her. Julie started to feel better. She smiled as she said, "I'll have a Coke, I guess."

The one lousy thing, she thought as she sat back with her drink, was that she wouldn't have a bike.

Unless there was a rental place in the little town near her aunt's resort—what was its name? Something to do with rocks or mines or magnets. Lodestone. Great name. She liked it. But she'd bet it didn't have a shop that rented mini-bikes. She'd just have to face a couple of months without one. Which was a first-class drag.

Got to stay in shape, though, she reflected. Running, maybe. Or swimming. Or hiking. Her hand strayed to the leather case that held her new binoculars—a last-minute present from her father, his way of trying to smooth things over. And a new bird book too, on Eastern Canada. Julie smiled. Birdwatching must have passed the ladylike test. Or else her dad had gone stubborn. Might be fun too, she thought. At least she could get off on her own with nobody to bug her.

She stared out the window. The sun glinted off a long slope of silver wing, half blinding her. Below stretched an endless snowy mattress of cloud; the earth had vanished. It was a strange feeling. If you didn't look out, flying in a plane was a lot like riding on a school bus. A big school bus that served Cokes and had a bathroom. But as soon as you peered out the window you knew it was no bus. The ordinary, the familiar was gone; the earth was now sky, with no fences, no roads, no horizons.

And no limits, Julie thought suddenly. Something

joyful stirred in her and she closed her eyes to keep the feeling longer, the feeling of lightness and freedom. Maybe birds had something going for them, she mused. *What if I'd been born a bird instead of a human? One thing for sure, I wouldn't have to worry about hanging up my clothes.* She grinned, then sighed a little. *If only Mom would lay off, let me do what I want. Why can't she understand I don't want to be another Roxanna? The world doesn't* need *another Roxanna. It probably doesn't even need the one it's got! Who the heck would want to be like her anyway? What a turkey! But then, maybe she thinks* I'm *weird. And maybe I am. But I'd sooner be weird my way than hers, and have some fun doing different things, things I've never done before. Even things that* nobody's *done before—*

A muted *ding* cut into Julie's conversation with herself, and the sign saying *Fasten your seat belts* flashed on. She straightened in her seat and cinched the belt tight, watching spellbound as the ground rushed up. With a soft bump, then another, and a howling *whoosh* of noise as the brakes gripped, the plane touched the earth.

2

A first-class villain

Julie unlocked the door of Cabin Three and smiled.
Good. The quiet old couple had left it as they had
found it two weeks ago. Clean and tidy. And they'd
never been a bother. Great customers. She looked
around. The screened window on the lake side was
slightly open and she hurried to close it. No point in
making it easy for the mosquitoes. Funny they'd
forgotten it. Propped against the toaster was a white
envelope with her name on it. She lifted the flap to
find a two-dollar bill. Well, well, a tip. Not a fantas-
tic tip, but still a tip. And all she'd done was bring
them soft drinks and ice a couple of times. How
about that?

She changed the sheets and pillowcases, put clean
towels in the little two-piece bathroom, did a quick
mop job on the kitchen floor and was turning to go
when something caught her eye. She stopped and
scanned the room. No, it wasn't something, it was

the *absence* of something. Over the big rough-stone fireplace was an empty spot that didn't belong. What was missing? The loon! The stuffed loon she admired so much. She had never dreamt that loons were such big birds, the markings so starkly black and white, the feathers so strong and delicate at once.

They had taken the loon. The quiet old couple were crooks and they had swiped the loon, for crying out loud! She fingered the two-dollar bill in her pocket. Did they mean that as payment? Even if you could put a price on it, the loon was worth a hundred times that. She felt as angry as if she herself had been robbed, angry because she'd been nice to them, because they'd fooled her, smiling all the time and then stealing stuff. And leaving her two dollars!

She locked the door and hurried through the stand of red pines towards the office. She'd have to tell her aunt right away. Maybe they could call the police and get the loon back somehow.

She stopped abruptly. Near the gas pumps stood a big bike, scarlet and silver and gleaming black. She walked over to it as if drawn by a magnet. A Honda XL 185. Zow! Looked like the latest model too. Very pretty. Her hand reached out to touch the red arch of the fender, high and proud over the front knobby. She looked around. Nobody in sight.

Wouldn't hurt just to sit on it. She heaved her leg over and bounced gently on the black leather seat. Nice! A little big for her, but nice. A great machine. Wonder who owns it? Julie thought. Maybe if I get to know him—or her—I can wangle a ride. She flexed the handgrips carefully, then sighed. This would be great country for biking. For the hundredth time she longed for her little Mohawk. She sighed again. Just a few more weeks.

Reluctantly she eased herself off the bike and went into the office. Oh-oh, something was wrong. Aunt Mo sat at the desk staring at a typewritten letter, her eyes holding a hint of tears. Her mouth was thin and drawn down at the corners, making her look almost old. Her hand plucked absently at her short red hair.

"What's wrong, Aunt Mo?"

Her aunt looked up. "I'm mad, Julie, that's what's wrong! Mad clear through! This"—she held the letter between her thumb and forefinger as if it were something dirty—"this is a letter from a creature who's been masquerading as a gentleman. He wants five thousand dollars by September. Cecil Purdy is the richest man in the township, he holds the mortgage on Three Loons, and he's a first-class villain!"

Loons, Julie thought. This was not the best time to report the missing loon.

Her aunt continued as if she weren't there. "Five thousand dollars!" She laughed, a short, sharp, bitter sound. "And I don't have a tenth of it. After twenty years pouring our lives into this place—loving it. Tim working so hard it killed him ... " Her hands covered her face. Awkwardly, not knowing what to say or do, Julie reached out to pat her aunt's shoulder. "Two more years and it would have been ours, and now Cecil Purdy won't renew the mortgage. He's been wanting the land ever since he came—for a shopping plaza, of all the disgusting ideas!"

"But can't you talk it over with him, Aunt Mo? Make him change his mind?"

Her aunt turned towards her, and the planes of her face, stiff with sorrow, softened as she smiled. The smile was so like her mother's that Julie's breath caught with sudden homesickness.

"Well, I guess it's worth a try, Julie. Better than sitting here bemoaning the cruelties of fate. I'll go right now. Can you manage the pumps?"

"Sure. I used to help my brother when he worked in a gas station."

"Good. I'll take the truck and pay a polite visit to Cecil Purdy, the Ebenezer Scrooge of Lodestone. Much as it's against my nature, I shall bow and scrape and plead and generally play the powerless little woman. Anything to save Three Loons." She smiled wryly. "Who knows? If I remember my Dickens, the original Scrooge repented."

Julie walked through the door to the snack bar. The old Wurlitzer juke box was lit up, throwing purples and reds on the pale linoleum floor. Aunt Mo had picked it up cheap, along with a stack of 78's over forty years old, when a roadhouse north of Lodestone had gone bankrupt last spring. And it cost only a nickel to play a tune! A strange, sad song was playing now, the lyrics drifting mournfully from the cloth-covered speaker:

> Well, trouble, oh trouble,
> Trouble on my worried mind ...

Julie glanced at the customer hunched over the pinball machine, wondering why he'd shoot his nickel on a song like that, then shrugged. It took all kinds.

Her hand touched the bill in her jeans pocket. She couldn't keep it, not now. It was like taking a bribe, like being in on a dirty deal. It was really almost like stealing from her aunt. She went to the cash register, rang up *No Sale* and slipped it in with the rest of the twos. There. She felt relieved. It wouldn't help much, but Aunt Mo sure needed it more than she did.

Besides, it made up a little for the mean things she'd thought about her aunt before she came to Three Loons. Two Loons now, she corrected herself silently. She'd been sure it was all a plot cooked up by her mother and Aunt Mo to get her away from Steve and mini-biking. She didn't think so anymore —at least not about Aunt Mo. Her aunt really needed her help this summer, Julie thought as she tied the strings of the big white butcher's apron around her middle. With a pleased sense of her own importance she began to polish the already gleaming coffee urn.

The sad song died away. She looked over at the boy playing pinball. About seventeen, she guessed. Not bad-looking. Not great-looking either. Too skinny. Needs a few days of Mom yelling at him to stand up straight, she decided. She noticed a big hole in the back of his grey sweatshirt and resolved to like him. Any guy who goes around with holes in his clothes is probably okay, she thought, grinning. He didn't look very happy though. The lights from the pinball machine flickered eerily over his face, over the uncombed mop of hair—ordinary hair-coloured hair—that kept falling into his eyes. His lower lip stuck out and he was frowning and talking to himself. Finally he shook the machine with both hands, then hit it on one side with his fist. Bells rang in alarm, lights flashed and the machine went silent and dark. He gave it a kick with his unlaced Kodiak and turned away angrily. He slouched to the counter and stopped directly in front of her.

For a few seconds his fingers drummed on the counter, and the ring on his left hand made a rhythmic tap-tap-tap like a woodpecker. He stared at Julie, then spoke.

"You finally made it, huh? I've been hangin' around for half an hour while you goofed off in the back reading love comics or somethin'. Think you can manage a hot dog?"

Julie's mouth fell open, then snapped shut before her anger reached her tongue. Just goes to show you can't tell by appearances, she thought. This guy was unbelievable! Holey sweatshirt and all! Hiding her rage with icy courtesy, she asked, "And what would you like on your hot dog, sir?"

"The works," said the boy.

"You got it, fella," Julie whispered as she turned to the stove. Including, if I had them handy, ground glass and rat poison.

She slammed the plate down in front of him. "Seventy-five cents, please."

He pulled his wallet from a back pocket and Julie's eyes widened. It was thick with bills. He riffled through a bunch of twenties and tens, extracting a dollar and tossing it on the counter. "Keep the change."

Julie hesitated. Another tip. Another tip she didn't much want, not from this joker. On the other hand, he obviously wouldn't miss it. What the heck.

She rang up the sale and dropped a quarter into her apron.

"You're new."

"Not very," said Julie. "Been around for over thirteen years now." She regarded him steadily.

His eyes flicked up from the hot dog and met hers. "Funny too." He grinned. His whole face changed. The blue eyes looked bright and merry instead of brooding; the mouth looked gentle rather than sullen. Julie found herself grinning back. Maybe she should give him another chance. She shook her head slightly and raised an eyebrow at him, a trick she'd spent hours practising last year. "I figured you didn't know how to do that."

"What?"

"Smile."

He smiled again, a little sheepishly. "Guess I came on like a sorehead, huh?"

"Yep."

Then he laughed outright and Julie laughed with him. "Hey, do you suppose we could start all over again? My name's Colin."

"Mine's Julie. Julie Brennan. I'm Mrs. Flanagan's niece from Saskatchewan. Here for the summer." With mock formality Julie stuck her hand across the counter. Colin wiped his on his jeans, then shook hers firmly. "So now that we know one another, Colin, could I ask you a question?"

"Depends." Colin's face changed a little, as if he'd slipped on a mask. "What?"

"Is that your Honda out by the pumps?"

"Yeah. So?"

"Nice bike."

"It's okay."

Julie took a deep breath. Might as well give it a shot, she decided. "Could I—would you—would you let me try it sometime?"

"What? Are you kidding? What do you know about bikes?" He chuckled.

Stung by his surprise, Julie snapped, "More than you do, I bet! For your information, you're talking to the Grand Trophy Winner of the Prairie Mini-Biking Tournament! And I don't read love comics, I read *Cycle World!*" She stopped, out of breath, her cheeks hot with colour, angry at herself for bragging, angrier at him for making her brag.

"Okay, okay!" Colin stepped back, his arms raised to protect himself. "You sure have a short fuse, kid! How was I to know? I haven't met that many girls who are into biking. I mean, most of them..." His voice trailed off as he saw Julie's frown. "Of course, I could see right away that you're different," he said hurriedly. "Smart. Tough. Built like a champion." He grinned at her. "Right?"

Julie looked at him, her anger melting away as fast as it had come. She laughed finally and said,

"That's better. And in the future, kindly treat me with the proper respect!"

"Too bad you couldn't have brought your bike with you."

Julie liked him for saying that. "I wanted to for sure, but there was no way." She stopped, then continued. "My mom doesn't think mini-biking is all that great a hobby for a young lady." She made a face. "Which is what I'm supposed to start being. And which I'm not very good at so far." She did her eyebrow thing again. "In fact, I'm flunking out."

Colin nodded slowly, his face serious. "Yeah, I know how you feel. In a way I've got the same kind of problem . . . " He fell silent and waved one hand as if brushing something away.

Julie didn't answer. The look on his face warned her to keep her mouth shut for once.

Colin came back from wherever he was and said, "Anyway, Julie, I've got an old dirt bike you can use. A Suzuki 80. I mean, if you want to." He looked away from her and hunched his shoulders as if expecting a blow.

Julie was too stunned to answer for a moment and in the pause he rushed on. "It's in pretty good shape, two years old. Not as powerful as the Honda, of course, but more your size. Great on rough ground, goes with you all the way—"

"Colin, you mean it? You really mean it?" She

reached for his hand and held it in both of hers.

He looked pleased. "Well, sure. Wouldn't have said it if I didn't."

"Zow! That's incredible! *You're* incredible!"

Colin laughed a little. "Yeah, I've been called that before. And worse. So when should I bring it over?"

"Um—now there we've got a problem." Julie's glance slid away from his. "Uh—could we keep it sort of secret, Colin? The thing is, I'm—I'm not all that sure my aunt would go along with it. I mean, my mother might have said something..." She looked up at him sideways, feeling uncomfortable.

"Oh. Yeah. Gotcha. Well, heck, Julie, no sweat. I could meet you somewhere." He thought for a moment. "Do you know the old logging road just south of here? Near the big S-curve in the road?" Julie nodded. "I can meet you there," he said. "When?"

Julie thought quickly. It was Friday and weekends were busy. "How about Monday at four o'clock?"

"Great. I'll be there." He smiled.

Julie smiled back at him and said, "Thanks, Colin. I can hardly wait."

He turned at the door and waved, just as Aunt Mo came in. She brushed past him, and her face was cold and strange as she watched him go.

3

The dead place

"Do you know who that boy is?"

Julie flinched at the harshness in her aunt's voice. She wasn't sure how to answer.

"Well, let's see—his name's Colin, he likes old songs, he eats hot dogs with everything on them, he's lousy at pinball and he's got a super bike. I guess that's all I know so far," Julie said. Except, she thought, that he's sad about something.

Her aunt sighed as she crossed the room. "His last name is Purdy, Julie." Julie blinked in surprise. "Yes. He's the son of the man I just wasted an hour with. Who has a mind set in concrete and a heart like a cinder. He still wants a fortune by the end of the summer." A tremor passed over her features. "And that boy of his, with his boat, his fancy bikes, his wallet full of money, that boy of his helps him spend it as fast as it comes in."

Julie could feel her aunt looking at her. Nervously she started to polish the coffee urn again, afraid of what Aunt Mo would say next.

"I'd prefer that you stay away from him. He's strange and wild and always in trouble. Last year he was expelled from school. Half the year he played hooky, the other half he drove the teachers crazy. He's a loser. You'll have to serve him if he comes in, but let's keep it at that." Her face hardened. "Besides, I'm afraid I can't look upon him with a friendly eye—his father is about to rob me of my home!"

Julie went on polishing. So what am I supposed to say to all that? she wondered. Her face frowned back at her from the shining urn. Finally she stammered, "I'm—I'm sorry about the mortgage thing, Aunt Mo. But why can't you get a loan from the bank?" she added.

"Interest rates are too high for the likes of me, Julie. These are hard times." She straightened her shoulders. "But I haven't given up yet. If I have to, I'll try to sell off another chunk of land. Purdy's in for a fight!" She looked at Julie and smiled. "Anyhow, you've worked long enough for today, young lady. Off you go. I'll take over."

Oh wow, what a mess! Why did I make that date with Colin? Julie asked herself as she slung her binoculars around her neck. Shoot, here I am in trouble over mini-bikes again! Maybe Mom's right, maybe I should forget about them. Ha! Fat chance! Besides, it isn't bikes that give me trouble, it's mothers and aunts! No point in arguing though. I'll just do what I want and keep my mouth shut. I mean, she didn't actually *forbid* me to see Colin. It was more like a suggestion. Which I have now decided to ignore.

She glanced through the door to the snack bar. Her aunt was making tea for old Mrs. Wannamaker from across the lake, back from her weekly trip to Lodestone. "Aunt Mo," she called, "I'm going birding. Be back for supper."

Now to check out the spot where that beautiful little Suzuki will be waiting for me on Monday, she thought gleefully, hastening southward along the gravelled road.

It was hot. Her jeans felt like wet armour. But at least the mosquitoes couldn't bite through them. Swarms of them whined in the bush around her, away from the marina where the swallows and purple martins kept the population down. She'd read in her bird book that a martin could eat two thousand mosquitoes a day. Should've brought a couple with me, she thought, slapping at her neck. Deer flies droned like distant bombers and bumblebees hummed in a slipshod baritone among the wildflowers at the edge of the road. She picked out the scarlet of nodding columbine, clusters of purple heal-all, ox-eye daisies half a metre tall, lacy clumps of yarrow and milkweed blooms looking like small mauve mops. Crickets chirped deep in the grass, and at the far end of Wandering Lake a loon laughed and laughed. Julie had a sudden sense of the whole world surging with life. Joy rose up in her. She spread out her arms as if to gather everything in and laughed as crazily as the loon.

Then the sun seemed to explode in front of her. She blinked in astonished delight. A dozen evening grosbeaks had pelted down from the sky to stand in the road a few metres away. She didn't move. The light glinted on the pale green cones of their bills, and their bodies, fat, yellow and proud, rocked back and forth on twig-like legs. For a minute, two minutes, they pecked at the gravel with a watchmaker's precision. Then, as if all were attached to the same string, they rose in a golden cloud and vanished as magically as they had come.

Julie let out her breath. What a dynamite show! And all for her! She'd never seen so many at once before. "Evening grosbeak." She said the name aloud, liking the sound of it, the feel of it on her tongue. She was glad she knew the right name: somehow it made the birds belong to her, made her part of their secret lives. As long as she could remember, she had always wanted to know the names of things. Not knowing was like being a stranger in the world, walking through it blind and deaf. Naming made her safe, gave her a queer sort of magic and strength.

She grinned suddenly, remembering what she used to write in all her books when she was younger. *Julia Elizabeth Brennan* at the top of the inside cover. Then underneath, in an ever-farther reach of definition, *R.R.3, Murdoch Corners, Saskatchewan, Canada, North America, The Western Hemisphere, The World, The Solar System, The Milky Way Galaxy, The Universe, Infinity.* Writing that long, long address with her own name at the beginning of it not only made her feel very small and very big at the same time, which was rather strange and exciting, but also made her feel *connected.* Connected to all the places and spaces around her right then, and to all the people and things backwards and forwards in time. A link! "That's the word," she whispered. "I'm a link." She smiled, pleased with the idea.

Must remember to mark down the grosbeaks on today's list, she thought. That was another thing. The lists. She spent a lot of time making lists of things once she knew their names. She liked lists—they were tidy, straightforward, comforting. Mom would never believe it, she thought, but I am a very orderly person. It's just that I have a few problems with my bedroom.

She came to a wide, rutted path. The old logging

road. Turning right, she walked west. The earth was crumbly and dry under her running shoes, breaking off in powdery clumps in the coarse, yellowish grass. Everything seemed brittle and parched. She remembered that Aunt Mo had told her there'd been no rain since the first week in June. The water was low in the lakes and rivers, the fish had fled to the bottom, and the leaves were as fragile as the old newspapers in her grandmother's shed—the ones with the big headlines, *WAR DECLARED!* and *PEACE AT LAST!* Julie frowned. Too bad. A dirt bike was more fun in mud.

She halted and looked around. She was in a small clearing by the side of the road. Probably where Colin would meet her. To her right was a gentle slope, about as high as a house, thick with purple raspberry bushes and second-growth poplars. A narrow trail winding to the top was just visible. Julie looked at her watch. Almost five-thirty. She'd better get back. New people were coming in tonight for Cabin Five. They'd need towels and stuff. She looked again at the trail. What the heck. Why not?

It was tougher than it looked. The bushes were thick, their branches tangled together in a tight, ropy web that clutched at her legs. Slowly she forced her way through, shielding her face from the stinging ends of twigs, using the larger branches to pull her body forward. At last she reached the top, and flushed with heat, peered through a skinny stand of birch saplings.

She saw a dead world. Trees—or what had once been trees—leaned awkwardly against one another, naked of leaves and stripped of bark. Like a heap of rotted crutches from an old war, they stuck there forgotten in a swampy lake whose surface, still and green and thick, lay like a lid upon whatever waited in the lightless waters beneath. No bird called. No flower bloomed. No fish leaped. Even the faint breeze touching her hair seemed to stop where she stood and skulk back down the hill. The sun, only moments before a confident furnace, was in this place a timid candle, cold and pale and abashed. It was a graveyard.

Julie shivered with fright, as if there were some strange menace there. The death in front of her was not like the deaths she had known: the stillborn calf last spring; the gopher standing sentry at its hole for that extra fatal second, an easy target for her brother Jeff; the two ducks caught by an early freeze on the pond three winters ago; the funny little sharp-faced kid in grade four, Vicky Some-body, hit by a tow truck right in front of the school; Uncle Tim; and Grandpa Mahoney, killed by an enemy shell twenty-five years before Julie was born, now only a picture on the mantelpiece. All these deaths she somehow understood. They were all sad, of course, but each one could be explained. She knew their causes and could accept the tragic results. She was even, in a peculiar way, reassured by the orderliness, the logic of them.

But her mind recoiled at this wholesale death in front of her. It was incomprehensible, almost evil with its smell of mould and rot and its threat of scuttling, silent, nightmare things lurking beneath. It mocked her. The surging gladness she had felt less than an hour ago vanished as if it had never been.

She turned and stumbled down the hill. Without looking back, she ran swiftly along the road to Three Loons, vowing never to go near the dead place again.

4
Let's go, Champ!

Quarter to four. Just time for a fast shower, Julie thought, flinging her shorts and T-shirt across the room. She was sticky with sweat; she'd cleaned the cabins in record time. Zow! In fifteen minutes she'd be on a bike again!

She stepped under the spray, soaped all over and counted "one, hippopotamus; two, hippopotamus; three, hippopotamus" up to sixty, then turned off the tap and reached for her big towel. Not on the doorknob where she usually kept it. Hmm. She moved around the room leaving wet footprints in her wake. No towel. Then she remembered. It was still out on the clothesline where she'd hung it after yesterday's swim. Well, she could hardly go out and get it stark naked. Might attract the wrong sort of customers. She was almost dry now anyway.

She brushed back her long reddish-brown hair, snapped an elastic band around it to make a ponytail and started looking for her jeans. No jeans. For crying out loud, where the heck were they? Let's see, what had she done with them last night? She looked in the closet, in each of the three dresser drawers, behind the big stuffed chair in the corner — one of her favourite places for clothes. No jeans. Shoot! Had Aunt Mo put them in the wash already? She was a clean freak, it'd be just like her . . . Ah! Under the bed. How did they get there? I don't remember putting them under the bed, thought Julie as she dressed and raced from the room.

Then she stopped and came back. She picked up her shorts, shook them out, folded them and laid them away in the second dresser drawer. She picked up her T-shirt, slipped it on a hanger and hung it in the tiny closet. She closed the drawer and shut the closet door, then looked carefully around the room. So okay, maybe her mother had something after all. Maybe life was easier if you could find your clothes in a hurry. Maybe. Just maybe.

She ran out the door again and set off in an easy lope to the old logging road. She felt a little guilty. She'd told Aunt Mo she was going birding. Which was only partly true. She would watch for birds, but — well, let's face it, there were times when you had to suppress information. Especially if it would make someone unhappy.

She grinned, remembering when she'd first

learned that particular lesson. It had been at the Sunday School picnic three years ago. Roxanna had shown up wearing a crazy white dress, all frills and pleats, with a big blue bow hiding her fat stomach. And white shoes with buckles. And, if you could believe it, stockings! Stockings! Julie had stared at her open-mouthed, until her mother had said, "Doesn't Roxanna look lovely, Julie?" She had shaken her head slowly and answered, "No, she looks pretty dumb! How can she go in the wheelbarrow race in that nutty outfit?" Then Roxanna had screwed up her baby face as if she might cry, stupid klutz, and Roxanna's mother had said, "Really!" and given Julie's mother a dirty look. Julie had laughed. And then, she remembered now with a shrug of pride, she'd won the wheelbarrow race. *And* the three-legged race.

Later, on the way home, her mother had explained the difference between honesty and something she called "tact," which Julie quickly figured out was the word grownups used for "lying." She chuckled. Guess I just used tact on Aunt Mo, she thought; Mom'd be proud of me if she knew.

She ran along the road to the clearing. A pickup truck was parked on the thin grass by the hill. Colin leaned against his Honda nearby. Beside him, gleaming in the afternoon light, stood a smaller bike and Julie's eyes widened in pleasure. It was the Suzuki, the name inscribed in rich ivory enamel on a gas tank orange as fire. The leather saddle shone black and the chrome on the front forks and the sturdy wire webs in the wheels twinkled at her invitingly. A white and black helmet dangled next to the high orange arc of the front fender.

Julie let her breath out in a long sigh. "Oh wow! Colin, is this ever a beaut!" She threw one leg over and straddled the roomy seat, bouncing up and down in delight. "Feels great! It fits!" She laughed up at him.

Colin was smiling nervously. "You like it? Really?" He fiddled with the canvas straps on his knapsack, not meeting her eyes.

Julie looked sharply at him, caught by something in his voice. What was with this guy? It was weird. Here he was with piles of cash, with *everything*—imagine having *two* bikes, for crying out loud!—yet he seemed afraid people wouldn't like him. Or his stuff. On impulse she reached out and laid a hand on his arm. "Colin, I love it! It's terrific! And so are you for letting me ride it!"

His smile grew surer and brighter. Julie felt warmed by it, and she was more than ever convinced that Aunt Mo was one hundred percent wrong.

"Good!" he said finally. "Okay, champ, put on your helmet and let's go!" He swung onto the big red Honda and kicked it into purring life. "You know how to handle it okay?" he yelled above the rumble.

Julie, testing out the controls, nodded at him and shouted back, "No problem!"

He snapped on his helmet and wheeled slowly out to the old road. Then, with a spurt of dust, he darted away.

Cautious at first, absorbing the rhythm of speed, the grab of brakes, the thrust and balance of her machine, Julie moved behind him up a rutted path. As her eyes and hands and feet began to mesh more smoothly, she accelerated and caught up. Colin signalled to her and pointed ahead to a trail that cut across a thinly-bushed hill. They swerved in unison and in a moment were travelling along it. It bisected the hill and edged down in a curving sweep to a flatter trail which disappeared into dense bush five hundred metres distant.

Behind her visor Julie started to grin, then laughed out loud in sheer joy. What a great feeling to be back on a bike! Her knees hugged close to the frame and she hunched down as if she were racing. Wonder how good Colin is? she thought. Maybe I'll show him some fancy stuff. She gave the Suzuki an experimental shot of gas and pulled ahead. Colin caught up. She did it again. So did Colin, the Honda easily pacing her.

With a wave and a challenging smile, Julie turned up the juice and took off towards the bush. Whee! She stood up on the pedals, showing off, then leaned back till the front wheel left the ground. She reached the bush, lowered the wheel with a thump and drove on without slackening speed. "How about that, Colin?" she whispered.

The ground was spongy beneath her, matted and thick with brownish needles, pine cones haphazardly strewn on the surface, but she could still make out the trail. She slowed a little, alert to the danger of the slippery needles—knobbies or no, the tires wouldn't grip in this stuff—then zigzagged through the trees in a series of tight turns. The resinous tang of evergreens came to her, and the dusty green smell of sun on grass. Behind her she heard the deeper hum of Colin's Honda. He could have pulled ahead, she knew. His machine had twice the power. But then, she thought with a grin, I've got twice the nerve!

The trail led them upwards in a wide spiral which grew narrower as they climbed. Slanted slabs of rock pierced the ground, and the tall spruce and pine trees began to thin out. Abruptly they emerged from the bush into a broad, mossy plateau broken here and there with ancient stumps. They jolted across a rusted railroad track and skidded to a stop next to an enormous wall of stone about twenty metres high and banded with greys and pinks. Julie switched off; a moment later Colin did the same, and the echo of the blended roars hung for a few seconds in the sudden silence.

Julie pushed up her visor and smiled. "Wow! What a great ride, Colin! Terrific machine! Lots more zip than my Mohawk and it corners slick as a cat!" She patted the gas tank affectionately.

Colin was staring at her, shaking his head in amazement. "Now I see why you won the tournament, Julie. You're crazy, that's why! You could've wiped right out on those needles, especially pulling a wheelie! You're crazy!"

"Nothing to it, my good man, nothing to it!" Julie was pleased by the look in his eyes. She thought suddenly of Steve back home in Saskatchewan and said, "I had a good teacher."

5

Don't look down!

They rested for a few minutes, heads bare to the sun and backs to the cliff.

"Hey, Julie, you want to climb up? There's a great view from the top." Colin's smile was brief, tentative. "It's my favourite place."

Julie glanced up. "You gotta be kidding! Nobody could climb that except a fly!"

Colin pulled a coil of rope from his knapsack. "It's easy. Look, see those little grooves in the rock? I made them a couple of years ago. It's just like climbing a flight of stairs. C'mon!"

Julie felt her stomach tighten. "I don't know, Colin. I'm not much of a climber. Saskatchewan isn't exactly famous for mountains, you know." She looked again at the rock face jutting towards the sky at a frighteningly vertical angle. She didn't want to seem chicken, but heights had always made her nervous. Even going up in the elevator at The

Bay in Queensville left her with trembling legs.

Colin was smiling oddly at her. "Here." He passed her one end of the rope. "Tie it around your waist." He tied the other end around his own. "Now I'll go first. Watch what I do, where I put my hands and feet. Don't move to a new position till you've got a sure hold, and don't do all the work with your hands. Use your feet. I won't go too fast. Just yell if you want me to stop."

Julie's mouth was dry. "Gee, I don't know," she said again. "You sure there's not an easier way up?"

"What's wrong, champ?" His eyes were challenging.

Julie clamped her jaw shut and tied the rope around her. "Okay, buddy, after you." Her voice had an edge to it. Darned if she'd let him know she was scared! It must have griped him before when she was so good on the bike. She marched to the rock.

Colin swung up smoothly, easily, as if he'd done it a thousand times. His hands reached and gripped; his feet probed and clung to the near-invisible grooves in the surface. He was now two metres above her, the rope stretched taut between them. Julie took a big breath and lifted her right foot. Slowly, timidly, her fingers seeking the worn depressions, her toes arched like a monkey's inside her Adidas, she began to move up the face of the huge Precambrian outcrop. It seemed almost alive under her body. The warmth within it, captured from the sun, pushed at her skin in waves, in throbs, like a giant heartbeat. Sweat formed over her eyes, under her ponytail, in her armpits, and drifted downwards in aimless trickles to collect at her waist where the rope chafed and pulled.

Bits of quartz and feldspar, embedded in the rock for two billion years, blinked an endless message at her. She closed her eyes against the tiny flashes, but they popped up on the screen of her eyelids to dance a jagged, limping dance. Between her shoulder blades, in a spot she couldn't reach even if she'd had an extra hand or two, her skin began to tingle and itch and she gritted her teeth. A deer fly, curious and daring, dive-bombed out of nowhere and skidded off her left ear with a sizzle of annoyance. She wondered if a lizard felt like this, and wished she had a lizard's skill.

Must be almost to the top, she thought, looking down. Oh-oh, mistake! All of a sudden her stomach writhed and thudded as if she'd swallowed a snake. With boots on. Dizziness engulfed her and she heard herself whimpering. Her mind kept telling her she was no higher than her own house in Saskatchewan, but her body didn't believe it. Her knees banged into the rock, her hands formed desperate claws which gripped till pain shot up to her shoulders, and her thigh muscles, knotted with fear, began to quiver out of control. She sprawled on the rock, breathing its dust, unable to move.

"Colin! Stop! Please!" She struggled against the panic in her voice. Don't be so stupid! one part of her said to another part. She shut her eyes to banish the dizziness, and when she opened them, saw Colin's face in front of her.

His voice was soft. "Hey, calm down, kid! It's okay, it's okay!"

"What do you mean, it's okay?" she croaked. "And what have you done with the rope?" The question was a tinny squeak. Colin pointed upwards. His end of the rope was tied around the roots of a scraggy pine growing straight out of the rock, nourished only by air and luck. Without any safeguard he stood beside her, as nonchalantly as if he were on a city sidewalk.

"Okay, Julie, now listen and do exactly what I tell you. Move your right hand up to two o'clock . . . a bit more. Feel the handhold? Good. Hang on. Now move your right leg . . . " Carefully, calmly he directed her, talking all the while in a quiet monotone, encouraging, praising, commanding her to do impossible things. And she did them, feeling the tension begin to seep out of her limbs, the writhing in her stomach settle down, the thick mist in her mind grow thin and vanish. She climbed. Two metres, five metres. Colin kept pace beside her.

"Now rest, Julie. I'm going back up to the rope. We're almost there—you'll be all right. And don't look down!" She felt his hand squeeze her shoulder, then watched as he climbed with steady movements to the rope. He fastened it round himself expertly, beckoned to her and began to crawl towards the top. Julie followed, and above her the blue bowl of sky crept slowly down. She mimicked Colin's careful moves, seeking the crevices, the tiny ruts, the little spurs of striated stone that spelled safety. Her hands were slippery with sweat. The ends of her fingers stung with it.

"Okay!" came Colin's voice from above. "Just a few steps more. You can do it, champ!" Julie fought against the urge to look down again. She wondered vaguely, briefly, about the sinister appeal of heights. She'd noticed it before in herself—on bridges, in tall buildings, on top of the hay wagon. Maybe it was because she lived on the prairies where earth met sky in an unbroken seam and height had no measure or meaning. She kept her eyes on Colin. Step, pull; step, stretch; pull, step, and up! She was on top, exhausted, panting, spread-eagled, face down on a blessed flatness of rock twice her length.

After a moment she drew a shaking breath and looked at her companion. "Why didn't you tell me we were going to play Spiderman?"

Colin laughed and flipped over on his stomach to lie beside her. Julie's heart rate slowly wound down to near normal and her breath gave up sawing at her throat. She reflected on how pleasant it was to lie still in the warm sun. She relaxed.

"Look over the edge, Julie."

Julie jumped. "Hah! No way!"

"Go on! Look!"

"I don't want to, Colin. It makes me feel weird."

"You turned chicken again? Go on! Go on!" He was yelling.

Julie raised her head to stare at him. His eyes had a strange light in them and sweat stood out in tiny silver drops on the hairs above his mouth. His lips were pulled back. Like Steve's dog, Julie thought. Suddenly Colin shifted his body, shooting forward until he hung far out over the edge, his long hair falling into space. Without thinking, Julie lunged to grab his shirt and for a second—a second longer than any hour she could remember—she found herself looking down, down, down, fifty metres or more to the ugly, tumbled boulders thrusting up from the shore of the lake. She shuddered and reared backwards, pulling Colin with her.

He turned to her, but did not seem to see her. His face was dreamy; he was somewhere else. "I think sometimes of what it would be like, falling through the air. I bet you'd feel free. Like a bird, a big white bird. All the things you were before wouldn't matter. You'd be *new*."

Julie shivered at his tone, at his strange, staring

face. This guy was really off the wall sometimes. "New, huh?" she yelled. "Only because you wouldn't have time to get old, for crying out loud! What a screwball stunt!" Slowly she unclenched her fingers from his shirt.

He seemed to come to and his voice was normal as he said, "I'm—I'm sorry, Julie. I didn't mean to scare you."

The view was as good as he'd promised. Below them, set like a jewel in a ring of forest and rock, lay a lake, translucent and deeply blue, its shining surface broken only near the shore where the breeze coaxed it into a slow, white-ruffled dance. The cliff, the remnant of a mountain folded in on itself as the last glaciers receded, stretched halfway round the north shore. Where the upthrust of rock stopped, in the northwest corner, the forest began. Tall red pines, bent but enduring, loomed like bodyguards in the crowded ranks of tamarack, spruce and tattered birch. A dozen shades of green jostled for room, and through that greenness, from the blue sky to the bluer lake, curved a cataract—a rushing silver braid of water that splashed and spilled from hidden shelves of stone, spinning gauzy webs of mist around the trees on its edge as it swept towards the waiting shallows below.

"I come here a lot." Colin's voice was a whisper beside her in the stillness. "That's Moonburst Falls over there, and this is called Big Rock Lake. Not bad, huh?" He was silent for a moment, then said haltingly, "I've got my own name for it. Darien. Do you know that poem, Julie? I studied it at school. Before they kicked me out, I mean." Julie shook her head. "The part I like goes:

> Then felt I like some watcher of the skies
> When a new planet swims into his ken;
> Or like stout Cortez when with eagle eyes
> He stared at the Pacific—and all his men
> Looked at each other with a wild surmise—
> Silent, upon a peak in Darien."

The words, and his voice saying them, made Julie feel strange—glad and excited all at once, as if she were shivering on the inside of her skin and about to learn a secret bigger than the world. The words called to her, promising grand and shining things; the joy she had known on the day of the grosbeaks sprang up again to fill her eyes and throat. So Colin was a namer too, just as she was! In a rush of closeness she touched his hand and turned to smile at him.

He didn't move. He didn't speak. His hand under hers was like the stone it rested on. His face was bony and grey beneath its tan, and his eyes were bleak blue slits. He looked as if he might cry any minute.

"What's wrong, Colin?"

His face changed abruptly and he jerked away from her. Julie saw him again as she had first seen him in the snack bar, mouth drooped into a cynical grin, features bland and faintly cruel. He stood up. "Wrong? Wrong? Why, what could possibly be wrong? My dad's the richest man in town, I've got all kinds of money, I can buy anything I want—you name it. I can even buy friends. I bought you, didn't I? Cheap too, for one used dirt bike! Right?" He was yelling again, and his echo screamed back at them from the silent cliffs.

Julie leaped to her feet, shock and hurt and fury warring in her green eyes. Her fists came up just as they used to when she was five and her brother Jeff was eight and he would kick her shin again and again, secretly, innocent-faced, under the dinner table, until in a blind rage she would lunge at him, only to be sent to her room without dessert, savage, unrepentant and sorry for herself.

Finally she choked out, "You crud! You miserable crud! What a rotten thing to say!" Her voice started to tremble and she stopped and turned her back.

She stood apart, seeing nothing for a moment, hearing nothing but her own pulse booming in her ears, until she felt Colin's hand on her shoulder.

"Oh God, Julie, I'm sorry. I shouldn't have said that. I know it isn't true, you're not like the others. It's just that—just that my life's sort of a wreck right now. But I shouldn't take it out on you. I'm sorry. Really!"

Julie swallowed hard. She remembered how often her own quick tongue had messed her up. Wanting to salvage the goodness of the day, to repair what this boy had nearly smashed, she said, "Well, okay. I accept your apology. I guess." She faced him and smiled hesitantly. "Now can you help me off this crazy rock so we can do some riding?"

His eyes lit up as he smiled back at her and held out the rope.

6

Probably harmless

Ahead of her Colin held up his hand and Julie braked to a quick stop, slewing the Suzuki around in a half-circle. Looking back across the lake she saw the great jutting cliff of rock—Darien now to her too—on which they had lain. Its other face sprang up from the lake's edge as fierce and enormous as a monument to some prehistoric god. Almost due south she could make out the marshy shallows of Sore Thumb Bay where Colin had stopped to show her the nest of a black duck, and close by she saw the thin silver twist of Hairpin River. They had clattered across on the weathered slats of an old wooden bridge which had sagged and swung with their weight, touching the tops of the rocks below— rocks which now lay bare to the sun, so shrunken were the river's waters. It had been a tricky run, but the little bike had behaved well. And so had she, Julie mused, thinking again of next fall's race. She turned to Colin to thank him.

He wasn't there. He was standing a few metres away at the door of a small log cabin almost hidden by alders and half-grown poplars. As Julie watched, he turned the knob and went in. She propped the Suzuki on its kickstand and ran after him.

"Perfect!" he said. "Perfect!"

Julie looked around, and then at Colin. "For what? Personally I don't get off on mice, spiders and slow rot."

"Nobody else does either, that's the point!" He strode across the main room to a small alcove at one end. Julie followed, picking her way past a squat iron stove layered with rust, a long table made of two planks hammered together and littered with empty bean cans, and the stuffed head of a deer which had fallen from the wall, its antlers spread out like the roots of a dead tree.

The alcove smelled old and musty and dank. In one corner was a disorderly pile of blankets and pillows, streaked with brown from the damp. Bunk beds with rusty springs stood stacked against the wall, and opposite them the doors of an old-fashioned wardrobe gaped open to reveal abandoned spiderwebs and a worn pair of rubber boots.

Colin turned and stepped back into the main room, ducking under the naphtha lamp hanging from a roof beam. He looked around, a tiny frown between his eyes. On the wall nearest the lake, which Julie glimpsed through the small dusty window, were two shelves lined with old cans and jars, a tin sink and a hand pump mounted on a square of rotting wood, with its thick black tail of a hose drooping downward and disappearing through the floor. Julie tried it. It didn't work. Beside the window, glued to a lacquered board, its eyes surprised in death and its ventral fins stiff and pink, was the biggest speckled trout Julie had ever seen, as thick as her two fists and as long as her arm. What a battle that must have been! she thought. Against the other wall leaned a tall cabinet made of steel and fastened with a loop of wire to discourage mice. From the shreds of paper and the droppings near its base it was clear the mice hadn't got the message. The whole cabin was no larger than the kitchen back home.

Under an empty can on the rough pine table was a yellowed piece of paper. They bent to read it. It was a trapper's licence made out to a Noah Clemens.

"Look at the date!" whispered Colin.

Julie peered at the pale type at the bottom. It read, *Signed this day June 25, 1940.*

"Over forty years ago!" she whispered back, then wondered why they were whispering. "You mean nobody's been in this place for forty years?"

She glanced around, wide-eyed. The peeling labels

on the jars and cans were strange to her. One read *Napoleon Bright Chewing Tobacco;* another, faded orange and white, proclaimed *Harry Horne's Custard Powder;* three cans of Campbell's soup in familiar red and white bore a picture of a kid with empty Orphan Annie eyes, a chef's hat and a big ladle. He—or was it a she?—smiled out at her and Julie unconsciously smiled back. A torn magazine called *Liberty* lay on the seat of the captain's chair near the steel cabinet. From the cover a young soldier stared into the distance, reminding her vaguely of her grandfather's photograph. She felt as if she'd stepped backwards in time. She shivered a little. Colin glanced at her.

"Weird, isn't it?" he said. "I—I feel as if I know the guy, don't you?" Julie nodded. "Noah. Noah Clemens," Colin murmured.

"He's probably dead by now, Colin." Julie was silent a moment. "And I don't believe in ghosts." She looked around apprehensively. "At least I didn't when I walked in here." She turned away, shrugging off the odd feeling the cabin gave her. "Anyway, you still haven't told me what this place is perfect for."

"For storing the Suzuki. We're only ten minutes from Three Loons." He opened the wardrobe doors wide. "Go get the bike, Julie."

Julie raised her eyebrow, but went out and wheeled the Suzuki back to where he stood. Colin wedged it firmly at the back of the wardrobe and piled on the old bedding till nothing was visible. "There. What did I tell you? Perfect!" He stepped back, shut the doors and held out the ignition key.

Julie didn't move. Her face was serious. "Colin, maybe we should shoot this whole scene again. I don't get it. I meet you five days ago, you act like a bear stung by a bee, then all of a sudden you're the nicest guy in the world. You dare me to climb a mountain, scare me half to death at the top, and now you want to play Santa Claus and give me a bike."

"So?" Colin's mouth looked surly and tight.

"So how come? You don't even know me. I don't know you. Do you give Suzukis away to strangers all the time?"

"Strangers?" He looked at her as if he'd just been slapped. "Well, excuse me, Miss Brennan, ma'am! Here I thought you were a friend!" His face was twisted in a mock grin.

Julie studied him warily. Hold everything, Julia Elizabeth, she said to herself. You'd better slow down. Before you get into something you can't get out of.

Colin spoke again, in a low voice she had to bend forward to hear. "The job's been vacant for a long time now, Julie. I—I don't have any friends." He flushed.

She gazed at him, stunned by his words, by the loneliness in them, and moved to embarrassed pity by his shame.

"For one thing, Purdy's not a popular name around here."

Well, I can certainly understand that! Julie thought. But she said nothing. This was definitely not the time to be a bigmouth.

Colin turned to stare through the grimy window, his shoulders hunched. "We're sort of outcasts, I guess. Ever since we came five years ago. We lived in Toronto before. Until my mom died. My dad got kind of strange after that. Kept saying you couldn't depend on anything but money, and you shouldn't get close to anybody because they'd let you down." He shrugged. "Anyway, he sold his business and we moved up here. Don't know why, except he told me once his mother was born around here. She died when he was little. Family curse, I guess."

He laughed without mirth. "For a while he watched me like a hawk, till I almost freaked out. Drove me to school and picked me up—in his flashy Lincoln, of course. The kids at school really got off on that. Then I ran away a couple of times. Stayed in the bush and had a great time all by myself.

"Finally he backed off and found a new hobby. Buying Lodestone. Just seems like he wants to *own* everything. And everybody too," he added softly.

"He sits in his castle up the road counting his money and figuring out who to rip off next—and tromping all over me because I don't want to follow in his footsteps. So mostly I stay away . . . "

Colin sighed and turned back, his face set in the bitter mould Julie had seen on the cliff top.

"But Colin, if your dad's that hung up on property, what's he going to say about the Suzuki?"

"Ha! Don't worry, he won't even notice. He only notices when I ask for money or get into trouble." Colin laughed again. "And I do both. A lot. So you'd better be careful, little girl. You're hangin' out with a dangerous character." He smiled oddly.

Julie didn't return the smile. Shoot! What a life! How could she be scared of him? Might as well be scared of a dog with a broken leg. With a rush of feeling, she remembered her own mother and father and how different things were for her.

Colin held out the key again. "Do you want this or not?"

Julie hesitated. "Just one thing we'd better get straight, Colin. If I take it, it's because I think we can be friends and because I had a good time today. Nobody else ever recited poetry to me, for one thing!" He looked at her swiftly, his face darkening. She hurried on. "I liked it! Really! And nobody ever called me Champ before, either." She grinned up at him, then sobered, her voice almost a whisper. "But no way, Colin, did you *buy* me. Right?"

Colin went red and stared at the floor. "I—I wanted to make sure—I'm sorry, Julie. I shouldn't have said it."

"Okay, then, it's a deal." She held out her hand for the key.

What a far-out day! Julie clung to Colin's waist, her knees gripping the cushioned pillion of the Honda as they headed back to the road. Yep, a weird day. And a weird guy. Maybe she was making a mistake. He'd had a look once or twice that was scary and wild. Sure was a mixed-up character. At least compared to Steve. Her mother would definitely not approve. She didn't even approve of Steve, so what would she think of crazy Colin? Julie chuckled to herself.

Then she remembered the other look too, the look when he saw that she liked the bike, and when he helped her on the rock, and when he recited the poem about the explorer. What the heck. He was probably harmless.

Besides, that Suzuki was neat.

7

Alias Prince Charming

"It's three o'clock and time for the news ... "

Julie picked up the full dustpan carefully and hurried to turn down the radio. With no one in the snack bar she'd had it at top volume to hear The Diodes belting out "Tired of Waking Up Tired." Great tune. An oldie, but a goodie. Her fingers rested on the knob for a moment. " ... as four new fires have been reported in the northwest section of the county. The weatherman says there's no relief in sight. The dry spell which began in mid-June is now entering its seventh week and authorities are worried that timber losses due to fire may be heavy. Area wildlife is also threatened. The local Natural Resources office is asking for volunteers ... "

"Hello."

Julie jumped at the sound of the voice behind her, and wheeled around. The dustpan hit the counter. Sand, crumbs, balls of fluff, pine needles, shredded tobacco and a dead moth spilled out to cascade down her T-shirt. Two bottle caps fell with a bright clank and waddled forward to stop near a long-fingered brown hand. Julie's eyes travelled from the hand across a dazzling white shirt up to a dark, tanned face. Her mouth fell open. Standing in front of her was the handsomest young man she had ever seen. In fact, he was perfect. He looked glossy and sleek and not quite real, like a TV commercial. Maybe he'll only last thirty seconds and then fade into *As the World Turns,* Julie thought, blinking up at him in confusion. But she hoped not. Tiny curved images of her own face looked back at her from the mirrored sunglasses hiding his eyes. She wished she'd brushed her hair.

"I'm sorry if I startled you." His voice was soft and deep, and perfect teeth gleamed in his perfect mouth. "May I trouble you for some iced tea?"

Julie gaped at him for a moment, half hypnotized by his face and voice, by the quivering bits of herself in his glasses. She wondered when he'd take them off.

"Uh—yeah. Sorry, sir, right away. Iced tea," she mumbled at last. She wiped at the front of her T-shirt and dropped the dustpan on her foot. Glancing swiftly at him, she caught the faint twitch of mockery in his smile and her face grew hot. She felt awkward and stupid and too young, and angry because he seemed to be none of those things. I bet he never had a pimple in his life, she muttered to the kettle. A weirdo. Another one. Wasn't anybody normal around here? Besides, she thought grumpily, he reminds me of Ken. Yeah. Barbie's plastic boyfriend. She pitched the tea bag into its little brown pot. One iced tea and she'd never see him again. Just as well too, even if he was beautiful.

Dimly, above the hiss of the kettle, she heard the hum of a bike. She peered through the window. It was Colin.

Her aunt appeared. "Julie, will you cut up these blueberry pies when they cool? Try to get eight pieces out of each."

"Excuse me, ma'am. Did I hear you say blueberry?"

Julie frowned. Why didn't he keep his mouth shut? Now Aunt Mo would be here when Colin came in.

"Why, yes, you did, young man." Aunt Mo was smiling at him and he was smiling back at her, almost bowing from the waist, where a white leather belt looped tidily through his crisp white jeans. Any minute now he'd fling a cape down for her to walk on, Julie thought sourly. And then her aunt cut a huge piece of pie. Way bigger than an eighth. Julie set the iced tea beside it with a clatter.

"Hi, Julie."

Oh great. Colin. Julie glanced at her aunt. Uh-huh. No more smile.

"Hello. May I help you?"

Colin looked at her, puzzled by the formality. He frowned, then mumbled, "Yeah, gimme a Coke." He drummed his fingers as she drew it, threw fifty cents on the counter and shambled over to the pinball machine. No marks in the manners contest there, thought Julie. His laces were undone again too. She wished her aunt would leave so she could explain things. She started sending out telepathic messages: Aunt Mo, leave the room; leave, Aunt Mo; there's a fire in the kitchen, Aunt Mo; Aunt Mo, the gas pumps have been kidnapped. It didn't work.

Sunglasses was still pouring on the charm at the other end of the counter. "You must be Mrs. Flanagan?" He smiled again. Must have a permanent-press face, Julie mused. "My name is Paul Craven, Mrs. Flanagan. I'm a student looking for work. Do you know of any positions in this area?" He pushed his glasses up to rest on his pale hair. At last.

"Well, now, let me see . . . " Her aunt fluffed out her hair, and her face relaxed again into friendliness. I don't believe this, said Julie under her breath. My old Aunt Mo, whether she knows it or not, is actually making a play for this guy.

She surveyed the smooth, clean hands and the immaculate clothes, and tempted by malice, murmured, "They need people to fight the fires north of here. I just heard it on the radio."

Paul Craven looked at her. His eyes were no colour at all, like chips of dirty ice, and what she read in them chilled her. As clearly as if he'd said the words aloud, Julie heard, "Butt out, little girl! Don't mess with me. You might get hurt." Then a veil dropped and the young man chuckled ruefully as he said, "Well, Miss Julie, I've had no experience in that sort of thing."

Colin was at the counter again, wallet open. "Need some quarters," he muttered. As Julie moved to the cash register she saw Paul Craven's glance fasten on the thick wad of bills Colin carried.

But it was Aunt Mo who spoke, in a voice brittle and unfamiliar. "You spend your money as fast as your father steals it, don't you? Oh, well, it's nice to get something back from the Purdy family." She turned and strode through the door to the office.

Colin stood rigid, his lips white with shock. His face went red, then pale. He looked at the wallet in his hand and hurriedly jammed it into his pocket. He scooped up the quarters without looking at anyone and silently turned again to the pinball machine. Paul Craven moved to a table nearby, a small smile playing around his mouth.

Julie clutched at the cash register. She felt terrible. How could Aunt Mo have said such a thing? It wasn't Colin's fault his father was a louse. What a mess! Her stomach knotted with tension. Finally she ducked under the counter and scurried over to Colin's side. He didn't look at her.

"Colin, listen. I'm sorry about what my aunt said."

Savagely Colin hit the side of the machine. There was a ripple of soft *pongs* and the screen lit up. Luke Skywalker sprang from a sparkling galaxy with lasers blasting, and R2D2 blazed like a Christmas tree. "Colin! Stop for a sec and let me explain!"

He turned and stared down at her. "I just won a free game. Sorry to rip you off like that. Here's your quarter."

Julie pushed his hand away. "Aw, Colin, don't talk that way. The problem is that your father owns the mortgage on Three Loons and he told Aunt Mo he wanted the money. Five thousand bucks, for crying out loud! By the end of the summer! There's no way she can do it. So she took it out on you." Julie paused for breath. "And—and that's why I acted so weird when you came in, because—because —Aunt Mo doesn't think I should be friends with you." She gazed at him, her eyes wide and bright, half afraid of what he might do.

"Yeah?" Colin's body was still. His arms hung from his shoulders as if they were made of wood. "Maybe she's right, Julie. Maybe you'd better listen to her." His voice was a grey sound.

"No!" Julie touched his arm, but he pulled

roughly away, jerking his thumb towards the front of the room.

"You got a customer."

An old man stood near the counter, his back bent under the weight of an old-fashioned canvas knapsack. With a frantic last look at Colin, Julie darted over.

"I'm looking for Mrs. Flanagan," the stranger said. He shifted a fishing-rod case from his right hand to his left and smiled, the lines in his weathered face crinkling all the way up to his eyes which were a clear and brilliant blue, nearly as bright as Colin's. He had the look of someone who had lived outdoors, away from cities and in solitude. He rested easily in his own body, which was slim, hard and corded with muscles in the shoulders and arms. His thick white hair was trimmed close around his ears.

"Mrs. Flanagan?" he said again.

Julie dragged her thoughts away from Colin. "Yes, sir, come this way, please." She led him through to the office where her aunt sat slumped at the desk staring at a bill stamped *PAST DUE*.

"Aunt Mo, a gentleman to see you," she said in a rush, then dashed back to the snack bar. A swell of music met her. Colin was playing that song again, the old one, the sad one. "Trouble in mind," a man wailed against a muted cornet, "I'm blue . . . " She looked across the room to where he leaned against the Wurlitzer. Trouble in mind. Yeah, well, he sure had that, Julie thought, wiping away a crumb of pastry left by Prince Paul Charming Craven.

As the last mournful chord faded, Paul walked over to Colin and said something. Colin laughed. Julie moved closer, pretending to check the salt and pepper shakers on the two tables near the door.

"You looking for a job?" Colin asked.

"Yeah. I'm flat broke," answered Paul.

"My dad wants somebody to fix the wharf at our place. You any good at that?"

Oh no, Julie thought, for reasons she couldn't explain to herself.

" . . . sure like to give it a shot," Paul was saying.

"Well, come on then, let's go."

Julie watched, the salt shaker forgotten in her fist, as Paul slapped Colin on the shoulder and said, "Hey, glad I met you! I can sure use a friend right now!" He'd said the magic word, she thought as she saw Colin's face. He looked happy, happier than she'd ever seen him.

"Colin!" Quickly she moved to block their exit. "Hold on a sec! Will—will I see you tomorrow as usual? I mean, we just started laying out that run . . ."

Colin stared at her without expression. "I think I'm busy, kid." He glanced at Paul. "But you can use the bike, if that's what you're worried about. I'll see ya." He brushed past her. Paul followed. The little smile was back, twisting the corners of his mouth. Once more the sunglasses covered his eyes.

"Creep!" whispered Julie, not sure if she meant Colin or Paul. Or both. She slammed the shaker down on the table. If Colin was that touchy and that stupid he wasn't worth thinking about. Besides, he was a meanmouth. And it wasn't even her fault. What a mess! She swallowed the sudden lump in her throat, half anger, half tears. And what's more, the other creep hadn't paid for his tea!

"So you're home again after forty years!" Aunt Mo came through from the back with the white-haired gentleman. "Oh, Julie, this is Mr. Clemens."

Julie nodded. "Hello, Mr. Clemens." Clemens? Clemens? Wasn't that the name on the trapper's licence?

"He'll be renting the cabin over by Big Rock Lake for a while. But first it needs a good cleaning. Would you go along to help? I'll take over here."

Julie's thoughts reeled. Oh boy. Terrific. The end of a perfect day. And just how could she talk her way out of this one?

8
Dear Julie

Maybe she should try the truth, Julie thought as she swept down the last of the cobwebs. Might be an interesting change.

She looked sideways at Mr. Clemens, busy scrubbing out the steel cabinet. He'd said hardly a word in two hours. Which was fine with her. The less said the better right now. She decided she liked him. He was peaceful. And he knew about birds. On the way down the trail to the cabin he had halted suddenly, put out an arm to stop her and pointed. Not far from them, on a clumpy bush lit by the sun, was a bird so brightly, so impossibly blue that she could only gasp. It was as if a piece of the sky had fallen down just for her. They had stood gazing for a full minute in the warm afternoon sun until, with a cascade of sharp double notes, the blue bird darted into the underbrush.

"What was it?" whispered Julie, needing to know.

"Indigo bunting," said Mr. Clemens softly. "So they still come."

Indigo bunting. What a name. What a bird. Julie said it over and over to herself. She would never forget the sight of that blueness, never forget standing there in the sun with the quiet brown gentleman.

She parked the broom and took a deep breath. What the heck. Might as well get it over with. He'd find out any minute now anyway.

"Uh—Mr. Clemens, I have to tell you something."

He turned from the cabinet where he had just set a silver-framed picture of a girl, and bent his head politely. "Yes?"

Julie opened her mouth but nothing came out. She swallowed, then blurted out, "Oh, shoot! I'll show you instead!"

She marched to the wardrobe, yanked open its doors and pulled out the pile of mildewed blankets. "See that bike? I borrowed it from—from a friend. I hid it here so my aunt won't know I have it, 'cause if she knows she might tell my mother and my mother sent me here from Saskatchewan so I'd get over being a mini-bike freak, and if my aunt finds out who gave the bike to me she'll have a fit because it's the son of the man who has the mortgage on Three Loons and he wants his money right away, which my aunt doesn't have, so she's upset and mad and told me not to be friends with him!" She stopped, out of breath.

Mr. Clemens was silent for what seemed to Julie a very long time. He frowned every now and then. Oh-oh, she thought. I guessed wrong.

"Your mother doesn't want you to be a—a—mini-bike freak?" he asked finally, and the corners of his eyes crinkled.

Julie shook her head and sighed. "She wants me to be a young lady. As if that's an occupation!"

Mr. Clemens murmured something.

"Pardon?"

He looked at her, smiled and said, " 'If a man does not keep pace with his companions, perhaps it is because he hears a different drummer. Let him step to the music which he hears, however measured or faraway.' "

That's more than he's said all afternoon, Julie thought. Sounds like a speech. Or something out of a book. Like Colin and his poem. "Let him step to the music which he hears . . . " She wished she'd said that to her mother.

"That mean something to you, Julie?"

She grinned up at him. "I think it means I can keep my bike here!"

He nodded. "You may."

She studied him for a moment. He was okay. He wouldn't fink. "Thanks, Mr. Clemens!"

Weird telling an adult the truth, she mused as she picked her way along the trail. They always *said* they wanted the truth, but if you went ahead and told them they got all upset. Mr. Clemens was different though. She couldn't imagine him being upset. She'd go back tomorrow. Perhaps she'd ask him to write down what he'd said about the drummer. Might come in handy. She reached the road and turned towards Three Loons.

It was dark for six o'clock. Towards the north the sky was veiled with dirty beige, a strange colour, threatening and unnatural. The fires, Julie thought. They're still burning. And not a rain cloud anywhere.

The air around her was suddenly thick, and she looked ahead to see a wall of grey dust moving swiftly towards her. It was Colin's truck, with him at the wheel. She caught a glimpse of Paul Craven lounging beside him. She stepped to the side of the road, her hand raised to wave. They were going fast. Too fast. The road was bad here, corrugated with ruts and sparsely gravelled. And stupid Colin was driving with one hand and hardly watching where he was going!

She edged closer to the brush. The truck didn't slow as it passed. She saw Colin's face, laughing, his eyes lit with recklessness, and Paul smiling that funny smile. She watched as the truck hit the curve without braking, watched as it skidded sideways. The left rear corner plowed into a row of cottagers' mailboxes and snapped three of them from their posts. The truck didn't stop.

Well, what kind of a screwball trick was that? Julie shook her head. Colin must be nuts! Or on something. It was that Paul character—he was big trouble. Shoot, maybe Aunt Mo was right. She'd better stay away from Colin. Not that she had a choice. As of this afternoon he had a new playmate! To heck with him. She turned into the snack bar.

Two letters stood propped against the ketchup bottle on the back counter. She grabbed them. Both from Saskatchewan and both for her! From her mother, ho-hum. And from Steve!

"You've had a busy day." Aunt Mo had come in. "Get something to eat and rest for a bit. You got your mail?"

Julie held up the envelopes and smiled at her aunt. Moving fast, she built a hamburger, poured out a glass of milk, took a piece of pie. The blueberry. She remembered who had eaten it that afternoon and almost gagged. Enough to spoil your appetite forever, she thought.

Upstairs, sprawled on her bed, she opened Steve's letter first. One page. She chuckled. He sure wasn't long-winded.

"Hi, Julie," she read. "How's it going? I got your

address from your dad when he came into the IGA last week. Kim and I are working there Saturdays, parcelling and stuff. I get $20.00 every week. Not bad, huh? I'm saving up for a new Suzuki, the 125. Pete let me test-ride one from the shop the other day. It's great, a lot better than the Honda on the trails. I won't have it for the Motocross in October though—even a demanstrator (hey, is that spelled right?) costs over 800 bucks! I'm practising a lot with Kim. He says Hi to you. Hey, guess who's hanging out with Roxanna Peters? That scumbucket Nick Adams. I figure they deserve each other, right? Well, that's all for now. Steve. P.S. I'll be glad when you're home."

Julie read the P.S. again, and her eyes blurred a little. Boy, she'd be just as glad, gladder even. Especially now.

She picked up the other letter. "Dear Julie." The small, tidy handwriting spoke silently to her. It *looked* like her mother, Julie reflected. Nothing wasted, the words marching across the page, straight and orderly, saying what needed to be said. No exclamation points, no spelling mistakes ever, nothing crossed out. She sighed, wondering for a moment how it would feel to be so—so certain all the time. " . . . Last Friday night we all went to the dance at the fairgrounds. Jeff took a nice girl, Hilary Peters, Roxanna's cousin from Calgary"—Julie decided to fire off a note to her brother warning him about the streak of lunacy in the Peters family—"and Roxanna was there with a good-looking boy from your class whose name I can't remember..." Scumbucket, Mom. Scumbucket is his name, Julie whispered, laughing.

Her mind wandered back to last year at the same time, the same summer dance, the same fairgrounds. She hadn't wanted to go, but her mother had insisted. What's more, she'd had to wear a dress! And stupid sandals that hurt her feet! She'd stayed mad and miserable on the sidelines until Steve showed up and they'd gone over to Pete's shop to look at the new Kawasakis. She'd taken off her sandals and left them somewhere. She laughed again, remembering. Never did find them. Ha! No loss. Her Adidas were much more comfortable. But of course her mom had got mad. And had more or less stayed that way ever since. Julie sighed. Would things ever be okay again?

"...So Katie and I will be coming in the last week of August, and we'll all go home together." Oh, for crying out loud! Her mother was acting like a mother again! If she ever wanted an outside job, she'd make a great spy. Shoot. Why did she have to come down here? Less than a month of freedom left! It'd probably take that long to clean up her room!

She looked around. It wasn't too bad, really. Compared with her room at home, which her dad had designated a slum clearance project, it was almost tidy. She'd discovered it was a waste of precious time looking for her stuff all over the place when she could be out on the bike. So she'd got in the habit of hanging things up or putting them away. But it still wouldn't be good enough for her mother, she knew. Maybe the truth of it was that *she* wasn't good enough for her mother. Her throat went tight and she crumpled the letter. To heck with it. She'd go birding before it got too dark. There was a troop of cedar waxwings that gathered in the big spruce by the water just at twilight, she remembered. Strange creatures. They looked as if they were carved out of wood and then painted, like children's toys. Great comedy act too. Last night she had watched them passing a berry from one beak to the next, right down the line until the last bird ate it.

She opened the dresser drawer to get her binoculars. Not there. She pulled out the second drawer and the third. No glasses. Weird. She opened the closet and felt along the high shelf. No. Not under the bed. Not hanging behind the curtain. Where had she left them? She was sure she'd put them away. They had been in the drawer that morning—she'd seen them.

They were nowhere. Julie felt sick and a little scared. How could she have lost them? How could she have been so careless? And with her dad's gift? They had cost a lot of money. And she loved them, the instant magic of them, bringing so many beautiful birds to her. She was sure she'd put them away. But where were they?

For no reason she saw again Paul Craven's face in the speeding truck, smiling, smiling . . .

9

You talk too much!

Whuff-f!

Julie's breath was a small explosion as the back wheel of the Suzuki hit the ground. Better that time, she thought, dismounting. The trick was to accelerate about two thirds of the way up the slope and not lose your nerve at the top. Her jumps were getting longer and higher. She'd win that trophy again this year, she vowed. Even with Steve and Kim in the race!

She glanced at the sun. It was hazy and smaller than it should be. The smoke from the fires near Algonquin Park never stopped. A dirty grey tarpaulin seemed drawn permanently over much of the sky, and always a faint smell of burning wood hung in the air. It saddened her to think of large stretches of green trees vanishing, leaving only charred skeletons, silent and black, to tell where the forests had once stood. Well, time to get back. Snack-bar duty at seven.

She moved to mount her bike—and froze. Five metres ahead of her, head thrust forward from a thicket of aging brush and swaying heavily from side to side, stood a black bear. Julie couldn't move. She'd never realized a bear was so big. She could see its mouth, sagging half open, with two rows of teeth shining like the zipper on her sleeping bag. Loops of white froth hung from its jaws.

Bears. Bears. What do I know about bears? Will it chase me? Is it going to attack? Does it eat people, even people who truly love bears and who would never think of bothering them? Julie gripped the handlebars. Carefully, quietly she pushed the bike forward a few centimetres.

The bear swung its big head and looked directly at her. Small eyes, sharp, wild and mean, stared into hers. Julie's mouth went dry. A warm thick smell reached her, oily, unpleasant. She stood still. The bear stood still. For a second, five seconds, longer, Julie felt as if there were two of her, one stuck forever on this patch of ground, staring forever at a bear that forever stared back, the other floating somewhere among the branches overhead, coolly observing the drama below and maybe betting on the outcome.

The bear dropped forward abruptly, and as if an unseen thread had snapped, Julie leaped into the saddle and kicked the start. She roared down the trail, heedless of the twigs that scratched her bare arms, jolted by the rocks in her path. She looked back once and saw nothing—which could mean that the bear had run away, but which could also mean that it had circled round and was now waiting for her just beyond the next curve. Shivering with fright, she gave the bike more gas and tore at last into the clearing where the cabin stood.

Mr. Clemens came round from the back carrying a shovel. "Evening, Julie. Good ride?" He peered at her more closely and propped the shovel against the cabin wall. "You see a ghost?"

Julie's eyes were wide and darting. She swallowed. "Worse! A bear! Back there on the trail!" She swallowed again. "Nearly scared the pants off me!" She got off the bike and started to shake. Mr. Clemens put his arm around her shoulder and held her firmly for a moment.

"I got away finally," she gulped. "It had little red eyes and it kept staring at me!"

"Um," said Mr. Clemens. "Good thing you had the bike. Bears move fast if they've a mind to. Noise'd scare him too." He gripped her shoulder again. "All right now?"

Julie smiled shakily at him, her legs slowly steadying themselves. "Yeah. Glad you were here though. You think I'll be safe on the way home?"

"Should be. But I'll walk along a ways with you. Go park your bike."

Quickly Julie wheeled the Suzuki into its hiding place and turned to go. She glanced through the window and stopped in her tracks. What was that? Some distance away, half hidden by foliage, a huge dark mound loomed in the dimness. She blinked and leaned close to the glass. It was a pile of dirt! She could see the raw edges of a large hole beside it. It wasn't a bear at all! She snorted in self-disgust. She'd be jumping at her own shadow next, and checking under the bed at night!

"I'll be okay from here on, Mr. Clemens." They had come to the place where the bush was not so thick and the road to Three Loons was plainly visible.

"Sure?" he asked. She nodded. "Well, stick to the open and keep a sharp eye. One thing about bears, you never can tell what they'll do next." He chuckled and shook his head.

Julie stared at him. Well, thanks a lot, fella, she thought. Before your very eyes I will now move faster than a speeding bullet. She waved goodbye and set off at a brisk trot. Hey, God, sorry to bother you, but if you happen to be listening, please get me to Three Loons with all my arms and legs and I promise I'll aways clean up my room, I'll never lie, I'll learn to make chili sauce and I'll never make fun of Roxanna Peters again. On Sundays anyway. How's that? A deal?

He must have bought it, she thought as she hurtled through the snack-bar door at a dead run. A vague shape was suddenly in front of her, and she lurched sideways in an awkward hop-skip-jump. Too late. She slammed into the shape, which turned out to be a mean-faced man in green coveralls, standing by the pinball machine. A bag of coins flew from his hand, and as quarters rolled off in all directions, he began to swear slowly and methodically, without raising his voice, on and on and on. Julie listened in fascination. She knew most of the words, but she'd never heard them said like this before, all run together in a long string, in such unexpected combinations. And without a break too. She wondered if he practised at home every day.

There was a sound of clapping behind her and she swerved to see Paul and Colin at the table by the window. Paul was applauding, a slow, mocking rhythm. His eyes held no expression. Colin didn't look at her. She stuck out her tongue at Paul, knowing it was childish, then knelt to help the swearing man, her cheeks hot with embarrassment and anger.

"Gee, I'm sorry, sir. I didn't see you and I was moving kinda fast. Because I saw a bear and—"

"Is that you, Julie?" Her aunt appeared from the living quarters. "Where have you been? It's almost seven-thirty. And what's this about a bear?"

"I saw one! It was near Mr. Clemens' cabin, a big

black bear! Stared at me as if I was on a dinner plate! I ro—I mean I ran back to the cabin. Thank heaven Mr. Clemens was there." Oh-oh, almost blew it, she thought. "Then I thought I saw it again, but it was just a pile of dirt from the hole Mr. Clemens was digging. He walked part way back with me . . . "

"Comin' south 'cause of the fires," mumbled the pinball man. "The bear." Julie looked up, marvelling. Several words in a row and not a dirty one among them.

"Why is Mr. Clemens digging a hole?" asked her aunt.

"Heck, I don't know. It was deep though." She laughed. "Maybe he's burying a secret treasure or something."

She was aware of a silence, a sudden alertness, at the table by the window. She glanced up. Paul's horrible eyes glittered for an instant, flicked to Colin, and then were covered by the mirrored sunglasses.

The pinball man started swearing again. "Somebody's cheatin', Miz Flanagan." He held out an upturned hand in which lay half a dozen metal discs. "Some _____'s been feedin' _____ slugs into the _____ machine!"

Julie heard a smothered snicker. It was Colin. She looked at him steadily, her face grim. Colin stared back, defiance hardening his features. Finally he blinked and looked away, scowling at the wall. You dope, Colin! Julie shouted at him inside her head. What kind of stupid game are you into?

She walked over to the table, her pulse speeding up with each step. "Hi, Colin! Haven't seen you in a week. How come?"

It was Paul who answered. "He's been busy, little girl. No time to babysit." He laughed harshly.

Colin laughed too, like an echo. But he was nervous, Julie saw. His fingers thrummed on the table-top, the silver ring clicking on every third beat in the rhythm she remembered.

"Butt out, creep!" she said, without looking at Paul. "I thought you might help me with that course, Colin. I could use some practice. How about it?" She lowered her voice as her aunt passed by. "Mr. Clemens was really decent about the bike. He won't tell."

Colin didn't look at her. He looked at Paul instead. What is this? thought Julie. Does he have to get permission?

"Sorry, kid. Like Paul says, I'm pretty busy these days."

"Yeah? Doing what?" Julie felt herself getting angry.

"It's an experiment in private enterprise." Paul's voice was quiet and threatening. "Colin and I have started our own second-hand business, haven't we, partner?"

Colin giggled. He sounded stupid. "Yeah, that's right, partner. Keeps us going night and day."

Suddenly furious, Julie turned on Paul and spat out, "Oh? Has it got anything to do with binoculars?"

"Binoculars? Binoculars?" Paul's face was smooth and his tone easy and unruffled. He turned to Colin. "Binoculars mean anything to you, partner?"

Colin looked up at the ceiling, cleared his throat and recited: "Binoculars, also known as field glasses, bring far objects up close. They are useful in war, birdwatching and looking in bedroom windows." Paul laughed. So did Colin.

Julie was shaken. This Colin she didn't recognize. He was playing right to Paul. The way Aunt Mo had with the blueberry pie. It was as if he were under a spell, like one of those snakes that come out of a basket and dance to an Indian flute. She drew a trembling breath. "Okay, pal, thanks for the definition. Glad to see you can be a comedian. It'll come in handy if you ever stop being a crud. See ya."

She turned and walked through to the living room, holding herself stiff and straight. Her knees didn't buckle till she reached the chesterfield, where she collapsed, feeling faintly sick to her stomach. Soon, muffled by the wall and by the hum of the cooler, there came the final sorrowing bars of Colin's song. Julie lifted her head and listened: "When you see me laughin', it's just to keep from cryin'."

Why had he played it now? Was it on purpose? Was he trying to say something to her, apologize in some weird way? Did he know himself what he was doing?

Julie shook her head wearily. She couldn't figure him out and she was sick of trying to. Nuts. To heck with him. He couldn't get rid of me fast enough, she thought, once that Craven creep showed up. Now he follows Paul around like a dog on a leash. If he gets into a mess, it sure won't be the first time. He'll just have to get himself out of it. Why should I worry over him? I've got my own problems!

She got up and moved out to the snack bar. Only an hour late. Big help I am, she thought. She glanced at her aunt, still talking to Dirty Mouth the pinball man. Aunt Mo looked tired. Julie sighed and started cleaning out the fridge.

"Bradleys up at Wandering Pines got robbed. Third break-in this week. You'd better keep watch."

"Well, that would be the last straw," said her aunt. "At least we've been spared that. So far."

Oh yeah? whispered Julie. She glanced at the table by the window. They were gone. Straws and serviettes lay crumpled beside the dirty plates and glasses. She grabbed a cloth and walked over to clean up the mess.

The letters, scrawled by a ballpoint pen, made a harsh blue scar on the white plastic. *You talk too much, little girl. Be careful.*

She stood immobile for a second or two, then trembling, frantic, scrubbed furiously at the message. It was from Paul, she knew. Her stomach tensed and a shiver went through her. He scared her. There was something strange about him. He didn't play by anybody's rules but his own. And if she got in his way . . .

Nuts! What could he do? He was only a kid, a few years older than she was. She was probably imagining things. She'd always been good at that. Too good. He was just a blowhard, a phony. What Nick Adams would be like at that age, if nobody lynched him in the meantime. She'd be careful though. She'd watch out.

There! It was coming off. She shook more Old Dutch on the fading stain and rubbed hard. Better not tell Aunt Mo. She'd blame it on Colin anyway.

"Fires're worse too, just north a ways," said the pinball man. Boy, he's a drag, Julie thought. Just full of good news. "If the _____ wind changes, gonna be in trouble around here. Good pie, Miz Flanagan. See ya." The screen door banged shut behind him.

Aunt Mo sighed a little as she emptied the cash register. "Maybe that's the answer. Maybe the whole place'll burn down. At least I'd get the insurance."

"Aunt Mo, don't talk like that! Something will turn up! It'll work out!"

Her aunt smiled sadly. "The time's almost up, Julie. Short of a miracle—or a buyer for that piece of land west of Big Rock—by the time your mom gets here I'll no longer own The Place of Three Loons." She smoothed out the small piles of one- and two-dollar bills.

Julie stared at her helplessly. Shoot! That Purdy! What a— Her memory tossed up a few choice words from the pinball man's vocabulary. Like son, like father! No, she thought, pulling on her jean jacket, that really isn't fair. Maybe he's just mixed up.

She walked down to the lake, as she had each evening in the past weeks. Just before the last light left the sky there was always a feeling of rest, of silence. The lake, busy all day, was a dark, smooth mirror. The wheeling, clamorous birds had gone to roost. The sounds of motors, voices, chainsaws, the low thunder of planes flying north to waterbomb the fires—all were gone.

Julie sat on a huge boulder near the wharf and let the quiet settle over her. Across the lake the moon was rising, unrolling, as it went, a glittering draw-bridge, all pearls and diamonds, which spanned the black waters before her. The moon looked so *near,* she thought, and impulsively her hand reached out for it as if to pluck it from the sky. The familiar feeling rose in her throat once more, the victory feeling, made of laughter, tears and a strange longing. Bits of Colin's poem floated in her memory. She felt strong and sure and happy.

A low cry from the nearby brush startled her from her trance. *Weep-pr-weel, weep-pr-weel.* She grinned. No mistaking that bird. It introduced itself every time it sat down. Over and over and over, a real ego trip. She'd never heard it till this summer. No whip-poor-wills in Saskatchewan. *Weep-pr-weel, weep-pr-weel.* It went on and on like a machine. Julie started to chuckle. What a crazy bird! One night, for fun, she had counted its cries. After two hundred and ninety *weep-pr-weels* she'd been too bored to continue. She'd half-expected to hear "This has been a recorded announcement . . . "

She laughed again and went in to bed.

10

Purdy and Craven Enterprises

"Put some flour on your fingers so they won't stick to the pastry," suggested Aunt Mo.

On my fingers? Why not? thought Julie. What's a little extra? It's already up to my armpits. She grinned and shook her head. Who ever would've thought she'd be making a pie? In fact, four pies! She surveyed the top of the old cabinet. There they were, almost ready for the oven. The kitchen looked as if a blizzard had swept through it.

Boy, if Mom could only see me now! Julie Brennan, cook. Ha! And yet she had to admit it was sort of fun, like building something. Making something that hadn't existed before. There was more to it than she had thought too.

"Now press the edges together and brush the top with that egg white," her aunt said.

"Why do you do that, Aunt Mo?"

"Makes the pastry shine."

Neat, thought Julie. She made a tiny pattern of holes on each pie to let the steam escape, and checked the oven temperature. And away we go, she said to herself as she set them in and shut the door. She felt a little tense, as if she were about to make a jump on her bike. No turning back now. No way to change what she had set in motion. No way to cancel a pie. She hoped they were good. Tonight—tonight!—her mother would be here.

She glanced at her aunt. "That wasn't too hard. Kind of fun."

Aunt Mo smiled. "It's a knack. Most people fling the dough around like Silly Putty. Makes it tough. But you have a light touch."

Julie felt pleased. And then surprised that she was pleased. But just because you made a couple of pies didn't mean you turned into a Roxanna Peters. Look at Aunt Mo, for crying out loud! She could fix a drainpipe and drive a tow truck and gut a rabbit and shoot a deer and clean a carburetor. And also bake a great pie.

Julie thought suddenly that her mother was a bit like that too. She remembered the summer before last when Jeff had fallen off the ladder in the barn and a pitchfork had speared his leg. Julie had stood staring in horror at the blood, unable to move, while her mother ripped off her apron—that apron she seemed never to be without—to make a tourniquet, all the while calming Jeff, giving quiet orders to Julie.

She remembered, too, the year they were hailed out and had no insurance on the crop. She could still see her father gazing at the ruined fields with tears on his cheeks and his arms hanging limp. Her mother had clucked her tongue once and marched to the big garden to save what she could. Day after day she had worked, without a word of complaint: canning, bottling, preserving, and driving every week to the farmers' market at Queensville fairgrounds till the snow blew in from the west. And there had been the needed new boots, the winter coats and even a shiny silver toboggan under the Christmas tree. Somehow her mom had done it. And never bragged about it once. Julie sighed. Now if she'd just get off my back . . .

Whoops! The timer on the stove buzzed. She leaped to the oven and lifted out the pies. Hey, how about that? They looked like the picture in the cookbook! She smiled at them and they seemed to smile back. Not bad for a beginner.

*　*　*

Julie trotted across the old wooden bridge towards the cabin. She'd told her aunt she was going birding. Birding. She snorted. Fat chance with no binoculars. She was getting sick of lying. Well, soon she wouldn't have to. Her mother would be here and she'd *have* to tell. What would her mom say? Oh boy. She knew exactly what her mom would say. The Speech on Careless Daughters. Again. She shook her head sadly as the cabin came into view.

"Troubles?"

Julie looked up. Noah Clemens sat on the captain's chair in the sun near the door, an ancient spinning reel apart in his lap. His patient brown fingers were slowly unravelling the kinks and loops and knots in the tangled line.

"Oh, hi, Mr. Clemens. Troubles? Yeah, sort of. Old ones and new ones."

"Bad?"

"Bad enough. My aunt still needs a whole pile of money, I haven't found my binoculars and my mother's coming tonight, which means no more mini-bike. Generally speaking, it's the pits." She sighed and sat down beside him on the warm grass. The afternoon sun was gentle and soft, filtering through the forest in the southwest, lighting the top of the cliff across the lake where she and Colin—a different Colin—had talked so long ago. Absently she scratched behind her knee where a mosquito had bitten.

"Just things, Julie," said the old man after a time.

Julie stared at him, perplexed. "Just what things?"

"Things don't really count in the long run. People do. People you love."

Julie didn't answer. Yeah, well, she thought, I'll just tell my mother that when she asks about the binoculars. Or I'll tell her to go talk to the funny old guy who lives all alone in a cabin. But she knew what he meant. And he *was* all alone. She stole a glance at him. His hands were still and he looked far away.

"You got any people, Mr. Clemens?"

He turned to her. "I'm seventy-seven years old, Julie. All my folks are gone. But now I'm back where all of 'em once lived. Some days they seem close by. My mother, my father, my little sister who ran away."

Must be the girl in the silver picture, thought Julie. Wonder why she took off. Wonder how old she was. She squinted up at the old man. Wonder if I should ask.

As if in answer, Mr. Clemens continued. "Just a child, she was. Seventeen. And balky. Like you, Julie." He smiled a little. "She was twenty years younger than I was, and after the folks died I raised her. Or tried to. Kept the reins too tight maybe." He paused a moment, frowning. "Anyhow, off she went with a stranger one day and I never found her. Found her grave instead, down in Toronto. Husband and baby vanished, like they dropped off the planet." He snapped the reel shut and rewound the line. "And now I'm home."

Julie felt tears sting her eyes. What a beautifully sad story! For a moment she wished she could tell one like it. She reached forward impulsively and touched Mr. Clemens' veined hand. He looked down at her and patted her hand, then stood up and stretched.

"Well. Time to catch my supper. You off for a ride?" He pointed north. "Found a little trail along the shore there. Near where the black ducks feed. Should try it."

"Yeah? Okay!" Julie grinned at him and went to get the Suzuki. She was in the saddle when he spoke again. "Julie, about the mortgage. Don't fret too much. I don't fancy a shopping plaza as a neighbour." He nodded and walked towards the shore.

Julie threaded along the trail to the north in low gear. The bike made a soft, throaty sound, an unobtrusive rumble muffled by the liquid slap of water against the rocky shore to her left, by the whisper of leaves above. She felt better. She always felt better after talking to Mr. Clemens. Even though they never said much. Wonder what he meant about the mortgage? she thought. What can an old man like that do against a bandit like Purdy? Maybe there really *is* buried treasure in that hole!

The ground turned boggy beneath her and the

knobbies sucked at damp sand as the trail traversed a low point near the lake. She dismounted by a huge upthrust rock covered in raggedy grey moss, one of those that gave the lake its name, and peered over it. Two ducks halted in midair, wing tip to wing tip, and fluttered down like small parachutes to land with a soft, precise splash in the lake. Her eyes followed. Closer to shore, when the ripples had settled, she could see through the clear water to the bottom.

A lone bass swam back and forth, back and forth, flicking his tail almost angrily at each turn. Like a sentry, Julie thought, and then realized it was true. Below him, on the sandy bottom which he had earlier scraped clean, small clusters of eggs waved to and fro, laid by some female bass who had left the area. Dad's doing the babysitting drill, Julie laughed to herself, and Mom's out pursuing a career. Why not? She watched as he nervously, endlessly, patrolled, stopping only to lunge at the tiny, curious trout who came too near. Absorbed in the submarine theatre, she stayed on, feeling lazy and comfortable with the warmth of the rock next to her. Slowly the sun slid down behind Darien across the lake.

Her last day with the bike, she thought suddenly, leaping off her perch. Might as well get in as much as she could before the light was gone. Even now the shadows were long and blue in front of her. The trail led to the right, away from the lake, and she revved the motor a little. It was a good trail, about three metres at its widest. Probably used by snow-mobilers in the winter, she figured, but not much of a challenge for a mini-bike. It sloped upwards slightly, snaking through the bush.

She gave the Suzuki more gas and began to prac-tise curves, guiding the little bike from side to side, making the turns tight and tidy, then tighter still, cutting as sharply as she dared, gradually speeding up as the trail grew steeper. She fell into a strange, almost hypnotic rhythm, a smooth, unbroken pat-tern of motion that lifted her out of herself. She seemed to be skimming over the earth, not held by it, but released, her forward path certain and effort-less. Half in a trance, she glided through the bush, unaware of time or distance, joined in a secret way to the bike beneath her. The wheels became her feet, the handgrips her hands, the engine a second, powerful, beating heart. She had a sense of total control and of perfect strength, known before only in dreams.

Abruptly the dream snapped. A wire fence sprang up in front of her. She stood on the brakes and slithered through the tough grass till the rear tire jammed against a knotted gatepost. Shaken, she switched off and swung free of the bike.

"For crying out loud, who built a fence way out here?" she grumbled. The next moment she knew. Attached to the gate was a sign that read *PRIVATE PROPERTY. TRESPASSERS WILL BE PROSECUTED. By order, Owner C. Purdy.*

Good old Purdy the Pirate at work again. Seemed as if he wanted to put a fence around the whole world. She glanced beyond the rusty barbed wire, following the trail with her eyes through a stand of cedars. Their sweet smell, which always reminded her of chocolate cooking, came to her on the quickening westerly breeze.

She was tempted. It was getting pretty dark and her mother would soon be getting off the train at Lodestone, but she couldn't help wondering what was behind those cedars. Nope, she'd better not. Besides, the sign— Nuts to the sign. Before you can prosecute, Owner C. Purdy, you gotta catch the trespasser. She propped the Suzuki against the fence and covered it over with brush and old branches. Carefully stretching the two middle strands of wire apart, she slipped through.

Julie ran down the trail softly, silently, her Adidas throwing up little puffs of sandy dust behind her. The clump of cedar was hushed, gloomy, strewn with green shadows. Dimly, from a high branch somewhere, she heard a red squirrel swearing at a bluejay. And then suddenly she was through the trees, standing on top of a small rise. Below her was a cleared area stretching all the way down to the highway and beyond, to the shore of Wandering Lake. To her right, not ten metres away, leaned an old shed. Farther down the slope, surrounded by smooth lawns and flanked by towering blue spruce, was a white brick house. The Purdy place. Lots of money sunk into that, Julie thought, and her lips thinned with anger.

She looked around. Nobody in sight. She'd just take a peek in that old shed. She ran over. Padlocked double doors with two windows at the top, each with a dozen tiny panes filmed with dust, made up the entire front of the building. Julie spit on her fingers and rubbed the glass. Standing on tiptoe, she peered in. From the little she could see in the shadowed interior, it must once have been a stable. There were six stalls, three on each side, and a feed trough along the wall opposite her. Three of the stalls now housed snowmobiles. Leave it to Purdy to have three. Arctic Cats too. Coils of rope and old fence wire were slung over the boards of the stall nearest her. Just above it Julie glimpsed the outlines of a loft that hugged the slanted roof. Um. Fairly boring. She was about to turn away when a flash of brightness caught her eye.

She pressed her forehead to the dirty glass and stared. A shaft of light, angling in from somewhere above, bounced off a shiny object. She couldn't quite make it out. It was on the floor by a big black tarp that lay in a huddle near the trough. Julie spit on her fingers again and scrubbed till the window pane squeaked. She stretched up and squinted, waiting for a moment while her vision adjusted to the dimness. Two round circles gleamed at her like an animal's eyes.

Binoculars! *Her* binoculars, she was sure of it! Rage swept through her. That creep Paul! He *had* swiped them, the rotten— She shook the door handle and pulled. No use. It was a new padlock, she saw. But where had that shaft of light come from? There must be a way in somehow.

Julie stepped back and began to circle the shed. Ah! Towards the back, near the lower edge of the steep pitched roof, a round hole, which had accommodated the rusty chimney pipe that now lay at her feet, gaped invitingly. She gauged its width. About right. Good thing I'm skinny, she thought. Now how the heck do I get up there?

She looked around the clearing. A tall red pine stretched its ragged branches nearby. No good. The lower trunk was bare of limbs. Her glance fell on a wagon wheel, like those on the old hayrick at home. It lay flat, about two metres in diameter, the wooden spokes covered with a faint green growth. Fungi pushed up through the hole next to the hub.

She bent to lift it. Holy crow! Stuck solid. Need a pry. She searched near the edge of the clearing for a branch.

The shadows were deeper now, and in the east, low on the far rim of Wandering Lake, Julie could see the rising moon, a curled white feather in the darkening blue. Gotta hurry, she thought. Finally she spied a limb of birch, lately fallen, its toothed leaves crisp with death. It fit neatly into her hands. She ran to the wheel and levered up one side of the rim. There. Quickly she rolled it over the lumpy ground to rest upright against the shed wall. Good! Now up and in, and back out again as fast as she could. She reached up. Her fingers touched the edge of the hole. If she could just get a little higher. Toes pushing hard against the wheel rim, she held her breath and jumped. There! Got it! She pulled herself up until most of her lay on the worn shingles, and then heard a soft thump from below. She looked down. Oh-oh.

The wagon wheel rested some distance from the shed, flat, useless, unobliging. That kickoff had done it. Now what? She shrugged. First things first.

Grunting, Julie wriggled through the small opening to the floor of the loft. A faint smell of rotting hay, dusty and sweet, came to her nostrils. She took a step forward and tripped over a big, empty wooden trunk. Waiting a moment until she could see, she moved towards a ladder at one side and clambered down to the main floor. With one stride she reached the tarp, knelt and flipped it back.

"Whew!" She let out her breath in a long whistle. "Would you look at that!"

Spread out before her were transistor radios, silver salt and pepper shakers, a coin collection, three Barlow hunting knives, a tape deck, a tiny portable TV, four digital clocks, an old-fashioned gold watch and chain, a typewriter, a Shakespeare fly reel and two graphite rods, a couple of diamond rings, a string of pearls, two gold cigarette cases—and her binoculars. It looked like a pawnbroker's window. More stuff was piled in the shadows against the wall. Well, well! She had stumbled into the warehouse of Purdy and Craven Enterprises. Business was obviously booming, she thought, shaking her head in disbelief.

Swiftly she grabbed the field glasses and pulled the tarp back into place. Yep. They were hers all right. Tasco 7X, with a tiny chip missing from the left eyepiece where she'd dropped them on a rock in Sore Thumb Bay. She slipped them round her neck and turned to go, when suddenly she heard voices.

11

Out of the frying pan

Julie lunged for the ladder and scrambled up. It was Colin and Paul! Probably with another load of goodies. Looking around wildly for a place to hide, she heard the scrape of metal on metal, the click of the padlock at the big double doors. Frantic, she leaped into the old trunk and lay flat. Her breath was hot in her throat and her heart hammered so loudly she was sure it would be heard.

"Paul, let's quit." Colin's voice was pleading, worried.

"Ha! No way! Tonight's the biggie! Got it all planned. And I need you, my lad."

"Paul, I can't do it. I can't! It's making me sick."

"Listen, Purdy, and listen damn hard. You're in. Right up to your scrawny neck. Whose shed is this? Whose truck is that down the lane? Who was the guy"—Julie heard him laugh slowly, nastily—"who talked me into a life of crime?"

"What do you mean, Paul? All you said at the start was that we'd swipe a few things, then put them back later. To see if we could. For fun. I just went along for kicks." Colin's voice rose, then broke. "I asked you to quit a long time ago. I didn't know you sneaked out every night to rob the whole town blind. I didn't know you were a—a common thief!"

There was silence. Then the crack of a hand against flesh and Colin's sharp cry. "You son of a—"

Paul's voice cut in, low and threatening. "Not common, Purdy, not common. They've never caught me yet. Ten years now and the stupid law boys have never picked me up. Last night I robbed the outfitters in Rockfield with the fuzz parked right in front." He laughed again and Julie shivered at the sound. "That's where I got this." A flash of light was followed by a terrible explosion that echoed from the roof above her, from the walls around her, shattering the air she breathed in huge gulps. Wood splintered over her head and she saw in astonishment the scarred joist, the small round hole in the shingle.

That loony had a gun.

"Hey, Paul, wait a sec now— For godsake quit pointing that thing!"

"You're in, Purdy, you snivelling little crumb! You're in so deep you can't get out. You've already got a record and all it needs is a phone call from me for the big steel gates to clang shut. For a long time." The laughter again. "And who do you figure they'll believe? A punk like you? Or a perfect gentleman—just ask that old bag Flanagan—like Paul Craven? Which, by the way, isn't my real name."

"Paul—I thought—you said—you told me I was— I was the best friend you ever had!" Colin's voice shook with the pain Julie remembered from that long-ago day on Darien.

"My God, what a wimp you are, Purdy! Why would I waste my time with somebody like you? Now listen. And no tricks. First we go down to the big house, which I really hate to leave, you know— best place I ever hustled. And we have a little talk with your stingy old man. Then we get the truck and come back here to load the loot. You and me together, pal! And when it's dark"—Julie strained to hear—"we'll hit the crazy hermit for his stash . . . " The voices receded, the door creaked shut, the padlock snapped.

Silence. Dark. Julie lay still in the old trunk for a minute, two minutes. Her heart beat in her ears. Sweat dried on her neck and arms. Her skin felt cold. She shivered.

The crazy hermit. Noah! With a rush of remorse for her runaway tongue, Julie heard in her mind the accusing echo of her own words: "Maybe he's burying a secret treasure . . . " It was her fault. Bigmouth had done it again. She had to warn him. But first she had to get out of this nightmare place.

She pulled herself out of the trunk and looked around. It was getting hard to see. She scampered over to the chimney hole and peered out. A wind, straight out of the northwest, and oddly warm, rushed by her head. To the north the sky was still light, a hazy pinkish colour.

Julie looked down—and groaned. The earth beneath was black with shadow, but she could see the wheel where it lay some distance away. Holy crow! At least four metres down. Should she jump? Yeah, and break a leg. Lot of good she'd be then. She remembered the coil of rope flung over the stall below and hurried to the ladder.

The noise of an engine reached her. Too late! They were back. In a panic Julie dove for the trunk and lay still. Rigid, breathing in little shallow bursts and fighting the urge to cough, she waited for what seemed hours. Finally, once more she heard the door, the padlock, the motor—and then silence.

She leaped up and scrambled down the rickety ladder. Grabbing the rope, she clambered back up and tied a knot round a roof joist. A reef knot. The only knot she'd learned in Girl Guides before she flunked out on the housekeeping test three times in a row. Yanking it tight, she tossed the rest of the rope through the hole, trying not to think of what she had to do. If she did, she'd chicken out for sure.

Quickly, keeping her eyes away from the ground below, she climbed out onto the roof, grasped the rope and swung her body over the edge. She dangled in the air for a moment, stiff with fear, the rope burning her palms. Forcing her legs forward and bracing them against the shed, slowly, carefully she walked down the wall.

She touched down. The dear ground, the wonderful solid earth! She'd never leave it again, she vowed. If God had meant us to walk around in midair we'd all have little wings on our feet like that guy in the helmet who delivers flowers.

Trembling a little, she took a deep breath. Her eyes began to water, her nose to burn. She coughed. Through a blur she saw two things, two strange and unaccountable things. In front of her on the shed wall her shadow danced like a maniac ghost. How the heck, she wondered, could you have a shadow in the dark? The second thing was the answer to the first—the flickering light behind her. She wheeled around.

"Oh!" she gasped. The whole northern sky was washed with a misty orange light that shifted and shrank and billowed forth again. For a second or two she didn't understand. Hands fumbling, she raised the binoculars and focused on the ridge of pines on the upper slope. She pressed the zoom lens. Something flared right in front of her and she stepped back in alarm. As close, seemingly, as the end of her arm, a tiny flame appeared atop the most distant pine, blazed hugely in the upper branches, and then sprang to the next tree, greedy and red, swallowing as it went.

Julie lowered the glasses with shaking hands. Fire! Another forest fire! And close! Her eyes grew wide with awe. So this is what they'd been fighting all summer! She felt the wind, harsh on her face. That was it. The wind had changed and was marching—no, stampeding—south, driving the fire before it. In the way stood the Purdy house down by the highway, Noah's cabin and even, if the flames jumped the Hairpin, the Place of Three Loons.

Julie whirled, and half-stumbling over the dark, uneven ground, ran up the slope to the fence. She had to warn Mr. Clemens. Now two dangers faced him. A rushing sound came to her, stronger, fiercer, deeper than the wind. It was the fire. She knew now what was meant by the "roar" of a fire. It really *did* roar. A childhood memory floated briefly in her mind, from years ago when they had come to visit Aunt Mo and Uncle Tim. On the way home they had stopped at Niagara Falls and the same low thunder had filled the air, made the earth hum. It seemed odd, even comical, that fire and water should sound the same, should send the same signal of unstoppable power, of catastrophe.

She stopped at the fence, squinting to find the nearly invisible wires. Parting the strands, she bent and hitched her leg through. As she eased her body after it, something exploded far behind her. Julie lurched with fright and a searing pain raced from her ribs to her spine. She cried out and wrenched herself through the fence. Her T-shirt ripped and she lost her balance, falling heavily on the dry, lumpy soil. To the north she glimpsed the flames, fringing the ridge of evergreens like malevolent orange lace. A huge hissing sound, like the steam from a thousand kettles, pushed at her ears. Then another explosion tore the air and before her startled vision a tree blew up as if dynamited. The sap, she thought wildly. She remembered reading how heat could expand the sap and water in a tree until it flew apart.

She scrambled to her feet, aware now of the throbbing in her back. She touched it and her hand came away wet. Blood. Great. And her neat T-shirt, the one that Steve had given her, all ripped. Terrific. She jumped on the Suzuki and kicked it alive. The roar of the bike was puny and almost lost in the greater roar that drove her onwards.

The dark closed in. It was hard going. Her speed slowed to a crawl as she wound through the wavy aisle of trees. It had seemed so easy this afternoon. She looked at her watch in the light of the headlamp. Nearly nine. She was an hour late. Her mother was due any minute.

But no way could she go right home. She had to

get to the cabin. Hope I'm not too late, she thought, and fear moved in the pit of her stomach. She glanced up. A haze covered the whole sky. No moon, no friendly stars, no glowing Venus. Only the menacing, shifting, rushing grey smoke from the north. She spurred the bike forward.

There it was. At last. Light poured from the front window, silvering the lake beyond. She wheeled around to the door and cut the motor. Strange. The door was wide open, creaking a little in the wind. At the entrance a creel lay upside down, its flap open, its contents gone.

"Mr. Clemens!" called Julie. "Mr. Clemens!" She felt a tingle of fear. "Noah!" No answer. The door creaked. The fire roared in the distance. The night sighed with the death of many small things. Slowly, glancing left and right, Julie led the Suzuki in through the front door, then stopped in horror.

The cabin was a wreck. The chairs were overturned. One lay against the wall by the sink, the other, with a leg snapped off, leaned drunkenly below the stuffed trout. The contents of the steel cabinet—sugar, coffee, flour, salt, dried beans—were strewn all over the floor. The sugar made a crunching sound under the Suzuki's tires. A bottle of maple syrup had smashed and its bronze sweetness trickled slowly among the debris. Beyond, near the bunks, she could see bedding thrown about, and the wardrobe doors ripped from their hinges. The picture of the girl in the silver frame was face down beneath the stove. The tiny icebox was open and water dripped from it in a steady, indifferent rhythm.

And at the entrance to the little alcove the body of Noah Clemens lay crumpled and still.

Julie dropped the bike and ran forward. Lord above, was he dead? She knelt and stared with horror at the dark red stain on his white hair. Had Paul killed him?

"Mr. Clemens! Mr. Clemens! Wake up! Please wake up! Noah! Can you hear me?" She felt his chest. His heart pulsed under her hand, slow, measured, firm. He groaned suddenly and opened his eyes.

"Julie?"

"Yeah, it's me, Mr. Clemens. It's okay. Don't move. I'll get you some water." She dashed to the sink and worked the pump frantically. The piston squealed in protest, then water streamed out. She filled an old china mug and held it to Mr. Clemens' pale lips, supporting him with her arm. He was light, she thought. His body was hard with muscle, but thin and springy. He groaned again, swallowed a mouthful of water and sat upright, a puzzled look on his face.

"Two boys were here. When I came in from fishing they were tearing the place apart." He shook his head as if to clear it. "One had a gun. He kept it aimed at the other one."

"Yeah, I know, Mr. Clemens, I know all about it. But we've gotta get out of here right now. The wind's changed and there's a fire on the way! Fast! Can you walk?"

The old man looked at her, still stunned and pale, then struggled to his feet, leaning heavily on her arm. His right hand was curled into a fist. He stared at it dazedly for a moment, then opened his fingers. In his palm lay a silver ring with a carved C. Julie gasped. It was Colin's.

She felt the old man's body tremble against her. "The ring! The younger boy—I grabbed him when I fell. He was wearing it. How—Where—" He turned and clutched Julie's shoulder until she winced. "Who is he, Julie?" His face was grey and the blood oozing from his scalp looked purple.

She choked out the name: "Colin Purdy."

He lurched away from her and lifted the silver picture from the floor. For an agonizing moment he gazed at the young girl, hands folded in her lap, who smiled forever back at him. Carefully he tucked it inside his shirt.

"Mr. Clemens! Honest, we've gotta get out of here. Come on!" Julie pleaded. She could smell the smoke. She could almost feel it, hot and heavy in the night, moving towards them. She pulled the Suzuki upright and turned to go.

In the doorway, swaying gently on its huge padded feet, its small eyes red as flame, stood the bear.

12
Another lie

The three of them stood frozen in an eerie tableau. Once again Julie had that strange notion of time suspended, of a still place between the swings of an invisible pendulum and of herself split in two, watching. She was aware of everything at once, as if she had an extra, keener sense: her hands gripping the Suzuki, the muscles of her arms tightening, her legs bending with the urge to run. The shifting light danced off the bike, and from the corner of her vision she glimpsed Noah Clemens, stiff and statue-like. The brown wrinkles in his cheeks were drawn in toward his mouth like crooked furrows in a field and the blood was gaudy in the white disorder of his hair. The smell of the bear—big, black, overwhelming—came to her almost visibly in warm, rank ripples across the space that separated them.

Then the bear moved.

Julie jumped on the Suzuki and jammed the kick-start down with a brutal thrust. The motor roared. She gave it more gas and the roar grew louder, bouncing off the walls and roof. She grabbed the headlamp, forcing it up to shine full in the bear's face, and pressed the horn again and again, her hands slippery with sweat.

The animal halted, one monstrous paw raised high. The wedge-shaped snout waved back and forth. Staring at the light as if mesmerized, the bear brushed at the air as if to clear it of the strange thunder, and then lurched back against the door frame. Turning, it dropped to its four feet and ran off into the night, whimpering like a frightened dog.

Julie let her breath out. "Come on, Mr. Clemens! Get on behind me!" She felt his weight on the rear fender. Good thing he's skinny, she thought. Revving the bike again, she took off through the doorway. If only they could make it across the Hairpin they would be okay.

She glanced northward. A swirling greyness, blooming here and there with patches of brilliant flame, was replacing the familiar bush, making a wall between her and Big Rock Lake—a wall not of brick or mortar but of death and destruction.

Her knees felt the vibration of the loose planks on the bridge. The river was narrow here. Too narrow? Would the flames hesitate, flicker, fail at the edge? Or would they leap like fiery acrobats over the slender line of brown water to ignite the eastern slope? She pressed the gas harder, steering with a desperate concentration around and through the clumps of birch, the thick alders, the sudden obstacles of rock and rutted earth that sprang into the beam of the headlight.

At last she felt the safety of asphalt beneath the tires. Around the curve now. Down the slope. And finally the Place of Three Loons, every light ablaze, reared up out of the gloom.

She steered the Suzuki to the door of the snack bar and cut the motor. For a moment she just sat there, shoulders slumped, tension and fear slowly seeping from her muscles. She felt Mr. Clemens' arms fall from her waist and the abrupt release of weight as he swung off the bike. Wearily she did the same and turned to him, smiling.

"Hey, Mr. Clemens, we made it."

His hand was gentle on her cheek. "We did, Julie. I'm obliged to you."

Julie was almost bowled over as a small figure with copper-coloured curls hurtled out the door and clutched at her legs.

"Julie! Julie! We came in a big plane to see you! Why were you out playing in the dark?"

Julie started to laugh. She stooped to pick Katie up and was surprised when the laughter turned to tears. She rubbed her soot-streaked face against Katie's smooth cheek, inhaling the wonderful little kid smells of soap and spilled orange juice. She pushed the door open.

The snack bar was full of noise and light and people. Julie blinked in confusion.

"Julie! Where have you been? Don't you realize we've been worried sick?" Then her mother's arms were holding her close and Julie relaxed into them, swallowing a lump in her throat and trying once again to make herself deaf. Oh, Mom, she thought, I know you were worried, but can't you lighten up? I'm here two minutes and you start with the questions. Questions that make me feel wrong and stupid and selfish. But she said nothing. She didn't want to fight. And it felt good to be hugged.

"Oh, dear, look at you! You're filthy dirty! Your clothes, Julie! And your back! It's bleeding!"

Julie sighed. "Yes, Mom. I'll tell you all about it." Well, maybe not quite all, she corrected in her mind. "But first you'd better meet Mr. Clemens."

"Hello, Mrs. Brennan. It's partly because of me that your daughter is a little untidy." As Mr. Clemens explained, Julie eased free and looked around. From the radio on the counter an excited staccato voice blared the latest bulletins on the fire. A group of men and older boys sat near it, listening intently. The fire crew. Mugs of coffee steamed in front of them. They looked exhausted; their clothes were blackened with smoke and grime and their blood-shot eyes were ringed with soot. Like a bunch of raccoons, Julie thought.

The Logans, with their three little boys, sat at a table near the wall. Mr. Logan kept shaking his head and saying over and over in a monotone, "All gone. Everything gone up in smoke. Never saw it coming ... " Aunt Mo bustled around them, quietly getting milk and cookies for the boys, patting Mrs. Logan's shoulder each time she passed. Mrs. Logan was crying silently, her eyes staring at nothing. Their place was—or used to be—a few kilometers north of Purdy's.

Wonder where Colin is now, Julie thought with a kind of distant sorrow. Bet he's sorry he hooked up with that hood. Boy, he's sure in a mess! Especially with Mr. Clemens knowing about the ring. That part was her fault, she supposed. Bigmouth at work again. She sighed. Yet she couldn't lie anymore, for him or for anybody. Including herself. It was too tiring.

The screen door slammed and a man stumbled into the snack bar. The first thing Julie noticed was that he had no eyebrows. Under a film of grey ash his face was pink, whether with rage or pain or burns Julie couldn't tell. What was left of a white shirt hung in dirty strips from his back and his pinstriped trousers were rumpled and stained and covered with burrs. He staggered to the centre of the room.

"My house!" His voice was thin and hoarse. "My car! My son!" He looked around him wildly, his arms hanging limp as if he didn't know what they were for.

There was silence. The man looked around again and Julie saw tears on his face, steady tears travelling down through the sooty ash on his cheeks, making clean little paths behind them. For a moment no one spoke. Then Julie heard her aunt's quick breath and glimpsed a strange expression in her eyes as she moved swiftly forward.

"Mr. Purdy!"

Holy crow, it was Purdy! Julie saw Noah Clemens turn and stare at him narrowly. She stared too. So this messy, crying, pudgy little man was Colin's father. The villain. Hard to believe.

"Mr. Purdy!" said Aunt Mo again. "Sit down. I'll get you some tea." She took his hand and led him to a chair. He followed her, one arm stretched out in front of him as if he were blind, or fending off something only he could see.

He collapsed into the chair, still shuddering, and began to speak in broken snatches. "I was at home—in my office—just closing the safe—and Colin came in with the Craven kid. He had a gun. He made Colin take everything out of the safe—all the money

—I keep a lot of money there."

He stopped suddenly and stared at everyone, his eyes wild again. "And—and then he hit me with the gun—I must have fallen. I don't remember anything else until the smoke—I was coughing, choking—the smoke was all around. The house was on fire, the garage, the whole forest was burning. I ran and ran and then I saw your lights." He started to mumble. "Everything's gone. My house...my son..." His voice trailed off and the tears started rolling down his cheeks again.

Aunt Mo kept shaking her head, saying how sorry she was and how she never would have guessed about Paul. Ha! thought Julie. You should have asked me! And how could Aunt Mo be sorry, for crying out loud! Had she forgotten that this was the same guy who wanted to get his mitts on Three Loons? You couldn't help feeling a little bit sorry, but in a way it served him right, the greedy pig!

Besides, she was more worried about Colin. Where was he? Had Paul kidnapped him? Or hurt him and left him somewhere? She felt a cold anger blow through her mind. What a slime he was!

The screen door slammed again. Cripes, what a place tonight. Like a train station. It was a provincial cop. Under his arm was the stuffed loon.

"Mrs. Flanagan, can we use your tow truck?" Aunt Mo nodded, her eyebrows raised in bewilderment. "Accident down by the old logging road. Oh, hello, Mr. Purdy. Say, it's your truck. Went right off the road into that old poplar at the bend. Front fenders and grille are wrecked."

Mr. Purdy pulled himself up and took an unsteady step towards the policeman. "My boy? Colin? Is he all right?" He clutched at the constable's arm.

"I don't know, sir. No sign of him at the scene. Just that young fellow you hired a while back, out cold. With a .38 beside him and enough stuff in the truck to start a store." He held out the loon. "Including this, Mrs. Flanagan. Knew it was yours. We've got the fellow under guard at Lodestone General." He looked around. "May have to evacuate everybody to town, Mrs. Flanagan. They're setting backfires now in case it jumps the Hairpin. You'd better be ready to move fast."

So it wasn't that nice old couple after all, Julie thought. Sorry, folks. She wondered for a moment if she could take back the two-dollar tip.

"But Colin? Where is he?" Mr. Purdy swayed a little and slumped back into the chair. His hands covered his face.

Something nibbled at the edge of Julie's mind—a cry, a lonely melody signalling her, a woven strand of sound stirring in her memory. It was Colin's song. "Trouble in mind, I'm blue..." What was that other part? It was later on, in the second verse, she was sure. For a moment the lyrics eluded her, then came in a rush. "I'm gonna lay my head on some lonesome railroad line . . . "

She knew where Colin was.

She glanced at her mother, busy tying up the laces on Katie's shoes. She bent down and murmured, "I'm going to wash and change my clothes, Mom. Be right back." Ho-hum, another lie. I have a real gift, she thought wryly.

She ducked under the counter and stepped quickly to the back door, slipping through it without a sound. Bending low as she passed the window, she led the Suzuki across the road and plunged into the bush. Hidden from curious eyes, she stopped to get her bearings. To the south she could see the curve of the road, just beyond the trail to Noah's cabin. The police car was there, blocking any traffic, and the tow truck was just pulling up. Their blinkers and roof lights flashed red and orange against the dark.

No point in going that way. They'd stop her for sure. For two reasons, she thought, her mouth twisting. One, I'm a kid. Two, I'm a girl. Nothing worse than being a girl kid when you wanted to do something different. Okay then, which way?

She thought for a minute. It was black and shadowy in the bush. The moon was gone, swallowed by smoke. The glow to the north, where the fire still raged, was faint here, barely penetrating the dense trees. Hairpin must have stopped it, she mused, at least for now. From here she knew she had to travel south and west to Sore Thumb Bay, then around the end of Big Rock Lake. Simple. Yeah, but the way was far from straight. How not to get lost? She could follow the fire trail along the shore of the lake —the problem was finding the lake.

Julie took a big breath, strapped on her helmet, swung onto the seat and spurred the little bike into the dark.

13
It's no use!

"I should be there by now," Julie said to herself. "How can a whole lake disappear, for crying out loud?" She reached forward and adjusted the headlamp until its beam sliced through the blackness ahead. Trees. Just trees and the weaving shadows of trees, rocks and the climbing shadows of rocks, bushes and the flimsy, dancing shadows of bushes.

The lake had to be close. She felt as if she'd been on the bike for hours. It was slow going. She'd covered a fair distance, she knew, but it sure hadn't been a straight run. Every once in a while there'd been traces of a trail, or the remains of an old logging road, but not often. Not often enough. The light found a clear spot slightly to her left and she steered towards it, upping the speed.

Then abruptly, with panic bursting in her, she braked hard. The Suzuki slid from under her with a stomach-turning wrench. She hung on and slid with it—a metre, two metres. The ground was soft and damp beneath her. Her knee cracked against a dead stump and the bike stopped with its front wheels spinning in air.

Julie lay still for a second, her face in mud, mud that smelled of rotting things. Shakily she got to her knees, then her feet, the fear rising with her until her very teeth shuddered. She clamped her jaw shut and yanked the Suzuki upright. Her legs went watery as she looked out over the terrible valley, that awful place of death she had vowed never again to go near. She had stopped a mere handbreadth from the wicked green of the swamp. The beam of the headlight caught a movement on the thick surface, a long sinister *S* made by some creature that hid beneath the slime. Julie shivered and shrank back, the loathing and terror coming from some unknown part of herself. She could taste a sourness at the back of her throat and jerkily swallowed it down.

She took a long breath, then another, as she turned away to push through the trees. Omigod, what a place! And she'd almost landed in it! She shivered again, as if trying to shake free of a hideous cloak. Sternly she ordered her legs, her arms, her body to obey the command from her brain. Find Colin. She had to find Colin. Before . . .

At last a shimmer of silver appeared in the blackness. She went forward slowly till she found the pebbly shore and swept the headlamp in a wide arc. She could see trees on the other side of the finger of water that stretched in front of her. Sore Thumb Bay.

Around the little cove, then, and straight along the shoreline. She would make good time now on the fire trail. The ground rose higher and the tall pines to her left began to thin out, their trunks stiff and black against the lighter dark. Once she heard sounds far behind her and stopped to look back. Below her, near the swamp, were moving lights, half a dozen or more. People, she thought. With lanterns and flashlights. Searching for her? For Colin? She turned and sped on. She would not be stopped. Already the dread was growing. Then, without warning, just as it had happened that first day, she came out of the bush onto the rocky plateau and braked to a jolting stop. She cut the motor with a quick twist.

Silence moved in like a waiting beast, swallowing the last rumble of the motor as it echoed from the sheer rock wall in front of her. To her right she could see all the way across Big Rock Lake. Above the far shore a ragged shawl of orange and pink and red was thrown across the top of the forest. Or where the forest used to be, she thought. The light fell on the water and broke into bright fragments, and the waves flung them shorewards like coloured skipping stones. It's almost beautiful, Julie said to herself. But what a price for beauty: vast stretches of land scorched, animals and birds charred and dead, the earth made naked for years to come.

Ahead of her, beyond the two rusty stripes of metal that marked the abandoned spur line, loomed the ancient cliff of rock that Colin called Darien. Julie's glance travelled upwards to the dimness at the top. Her breath caught and a little pulse of alarm beat in her throat. For there on the very edge of that high, high cliff, stood Colin, just as she had feared. Once again the song rose in her memory, the song that had led her here. "Trouble in mind, I'm blue, But I won't be blue always . . . "

"No!" she said aloud, and the faint sound hung in the air. Mustn't frighten him, she thought. Or surprise him. She called softly. "Colin . . . Colin . . . " The figure didn't move. Far out on the lake Julie heard a loon and for a brief moment thought it was Colin answering, Colin crying a lonely, bewildered, grieving cry, cornered and lost in an empty dark place at the end of things.

"Colin!" she said again, the plea more urgent now. "Come down, Colin! Please!" Still no response. He stood there motionless, deaf, dumb. Maybe he can't hear me at all, Julie thought. Maybe he's too far away to hear anything.

Her teeth clenched as she realized what she must

do. Go up. Go up that rock. Without his help this time, without a rope, in the middle of the night, tired and scared and with her knee still hurting from the tree stump. She swallowed. Her spit was dry. Julie, for crying out loud, nobody has dry spit. Are you freaking out too? She marched grimly forward, her eyes seeking, in the light of the headlamp, those worn niches that Colin had made in the rock, her only ladder to the top. She reached the rock, stretched out her arms and searched with cold fingers for the first handhold. Ah! There it was. And there, to her left, was another.

Carefully, willing her mind to go blank, she stepped up, found a resting place and pulled her body after. Reach, find, pull. Up half her height. Again. Reach, stay close, don't move till you're sure, find a handhold, then a foothold, pull. Up. Up. Don't look down. There's only dark down there anyway. Dark and distance. A long way to fall. The thought hammered in her mind as she passed beyond the range of the little light from the Suzuki. The shadows tricked her vision and she could taste the salt of sweat as she licked her dry lips.

She reached up once more, found a rough-edged stone and hauled herself another half metre. The stone moved a little and her stomach knotted. Sternly she thought about something else, about Colin up on the top. She must get to him, talk to him. She leaned against the cliff's cold surface for a moment's rest. Her breath came in harsh whistles, as if she'd been running, and she could feel dampness on her neck under her hair. She moved one hand back and forth above her. There. And there. Now move your left foot, Julie. That's it. Now find a place to put it, idiot! Her foot waved in the air for a second, ten seconds, and then connected with something solid. She rested.

Abruptly the foothold collapsed, her left hand lost its grip and her face scraped cruelly against the rough rock. She hung gasping in panic, half her body flailing the air. She had time only to think "This is it!" as her right foot slid from its crumbling perch. Desperate, hanging by one hand now—a hand that felt as if it were being torn from her arm—she threw herself against the rock, scrabbling at it with toes and fingers. Swinging wide with her left arm, she hit something prickly. Like needles. She looked up. Silhouetted against the sky was the scraggy little pine Colin had tied the rope to. If she could just reach it . . . It was her only chance. If she could just grab it . . . She lunged up to the left and her hand closed over the rough bark of a branch.

She hung there, burrowing into the rock like an animal run to ground, her heart pounding so fast it hurt. She grew dizzy and her stomach heaved. She closed her eyes and waited. Slowly the tumult in her body quieted. Okay. Enough of that. Up. Her sneakered foot explored below and found a home. One hand groped above and clutched at a jutting chunk of granite. It held. Reluctantly she abandoned the safety of the pine branch and drew herself up. Up again. And again. And there she was on top of Darien!

For a long moment she lay trembling uncontrollably. Finally she raised her head. Colin was sitting not far from her, right on the edge, his head bent, his feet dangling in the black air.

"Colin!" She scrambled over to kneel beside him.

His face was still, his features lit with a strange and ghastly light. Julie glanced across the lake. The whole northern shore was aflame. The fire was leaping from tree to tree, sending columns of sparks into the air like swarms of fireflies, spraying the sky with geysers of orange and yellow and terrible pink. And all of it was reflected in the lake below—a giant mirror to capture and double the inferno. Julie was reminded of a picture she'd seen in an old book at the Queensville library. It was a painting of some long-dead artist's idea of hell. She squinted a little and the dancing shards of fire on the water seemed for a moment to be human figures, squirming, plunging, twisting to escape the torment. She wrenched her eyes away.

Colin sat unmoving. "Colin!" Julie touched his

hand. It had no warmth, no life. She took it in both of hers and held it, rubbing it gently. "Colin. Colin." She whispered his name over and over.

He turned, at last, and looked at her with a dreadful expression. His eyes weren't his own; they stared through her.

The words flooded from his mouth. "It's no use! It's no use! There's nothing left! And I did it! It was all my fault! It's no use!"

"Colin, it's okay, don't worry, everything's going to be all right!" She could feel his pain and confusion as if she were inside his mind, and she suddenly felt older than him, much older. She stroked his hand and murmured to him softly, again and again, "It's okay, it's okay," in the singsong chant of a little child.

A shudder went through him. "It's no use. He's dead and I killed him. The only person I cared about. Even if he didn't care about me. I killed him!" Tears ran down his cheeks in the eerie light and splashed on Julie's hand.

"Killed who? Colin, what are you talking about?" He must mean Paul, she thought.

"My dad!" He shook her off and sprang to his feet. "The roof was on fire. Paul made me drive away . . . " His voice rose. "I crashed into the tree and ran. I was scared, so scared"—he was screaming now—"and I left my father to burn!" He covered his face with his hands as if to shut out the memory, and his body swayed forward, dark against the fiery light of the sky beyond, teetering on the edge of the cliff.

Omigod, he's going over! Julie leaped up and grabbed him round the waist. The two figures clung together on the lip of the precipice, wavering as if undecided. As she fought to keep her balance Julie could hear the sharp, hungry lick of water far, far down. With frantic strength she threw herself backward, dragging Colin with her. They hit the stony ground with a bone-bruising thump.

She held on tightly and began to shout at him. "Colin, your dad's not dead! He's all right! He got out! You didn't kill him! The house is burned down but he's okay—except he doesn't have any eyebrows left!" Suddenly she started to giggle and she couldn't stop.

She felt Colin go limp, all the tightness in him uncoiling like a runaway fishing line. His breath was ragged and noisy in her ear. Still she giggled, then laughed out loud. Tears came too, and she was crying and laughing at the same time, but it was okay. It was okay. Colin was doing the same thing.

14

A different drummer

It was just past Sore Thumb Bay that they saw the fire. Julie braked sharply and Colin lurched forward against her. Thick smoke blocked their path, black velvety waves of it smothering the landscape, lethal, awesome and rolling steadily towards them.

"How did it jump the Hairpin?" yelled Julie above the growing roar.

"It didn't," Colin shouted in her ear. "Must be a backfire the rangers set to stop the big one! Cut to the right, Julie! There's only one way through!"

She obeyed, glad to let him decide, gladder still to hear the strength in his voice. Once again she focused the headlight on the few metres directly ahead, and once again steered through the evergreen forest, around rocks that thrust up suddenly before them—always with the rumble and swish of the fire following, always with the smell of smoke, of cinders, of burning pine resin in her eyes and nose and throat. She could feel the heat through her tattered T-shirt and jeans and along her bare arms, now bleeding from a hundred scratches and swollen with a hundred insect bites. Sometimes she drove blind as billows of black unfurled to cloak the ground in front of them.

Coughing, eyes streaming, they reached a place where they could go no further. "Okay!" shouted Colin. "This is it!"

Julie turned to look at him. He couldn't mean it. They were at the *dead place!* In the beam of the Suzuki's light she saw the mustardy scum stretch into the blackness beyond. She shuddered.

"Colin, you gotta be kidding!" She searched his face, hoping he would laugh and nod and tell her it was just one of his weird jokes. For answer he swung free of the bike and kicked off his boots. With hurrying fingers he yanked the leather laces free, tied them together and made loops at each end. Grabbing Julie's arm, he pushed it through one loop and slipped the other on his own.

"Let's go!"

Julie felt all the blood drain out of her head and settle in a cold pool somewhere in her stomach. "Colin, I can't go in there! I can't! It's—it's horrible! It's full of slimy things—I can't, Colin!" Her voice squeaked. "I'll die if I go in there!"

Colin grabbed her shoulders, shook her hard and

swung her round. She stared into a swaying curtain of flame whose wispy, fragile folds destroyed everything they touched. And whose path led directly to where Julie stood. She gasped and flinched against Colin as the heat pushed at her. The roar, the terrible *whoosh* of sound, set her body trembling.

"You'll die if you *don't!*" Colin shouted savagely. Scooping her into his arms he turned and plunged into the swamp.

Oh lord! Julie thought, recoiling from the putrid smell of decay.

Colin set her down and they started to walk, the viscous water sometimes to their knees, sometimes rising to chest height, the ooze sucking at their feet with each step. Julie stumbled after Colin as if she were a puppy on a leash, her mind gibbering brokenly as jagged images of ancient lizard-like things, older than dinosaurs, slithered through it. Once her shirt caught on a branch that periscoped up from the blanket of slime. She ripped it loose. Once she lost her footing altogether, slipping down, down into a deep trench. The muck closed over her head; the green scum filled her mouth.

Colin reached and pulled her to the surface. She choked and gagged and spit out the horror, and a tremor of nausea rippled out from her belly right to her fingers and toes. She lurched on, slowed by the weight of gluey mud that clung to her soaked jeans.

She felt a shoe go, sucked from her foot by some greedy mouth of ooze. She was certain each step would be her last. Swirling reeds, long strings of weed as tough as whips, clutched at her legs, wound themselves about her waist as if to trap her there forever. She pulled at them, twisting free, only to be snared again the next moment.

Then Colin stopped so abruptly she bumped into him. He pointed, motioning her to be still. The fitful brightness of the flames behind them touched the swamp with a smoky yellow glow. Through it, half-swimming, half-walking on all fours, struggled the bear. As they watched, the animal swivelled its great head towards them. For a few seconds the bead-like eyes glared in fear—or was it warning?—before it turned and plunged on. Colin plunged after it, pulling Julie with him.

"We'll follow the bear!" he yelled. "He's smarter than we are! Come on!"

They stumbled on through the flickering, eerie light. Julie's arms and legs ached with a deep tiredness. Dimly, from far behind them, they heard a loud *whumpf!* The bike, thought Julie. The beautiful Suzuki, blown up. She moved on, more out of habit now than desire. Her fear was gone; there was room only for weariness. She felt as if she'd been walking through the swamp most of her life and that she and Colin were the only people in the world. The lizard pictures came back with a rush and for a moment she imagined that the earth had just begun, that they had somehow travelled back in time to this strange place full of unknown creatures and unknown perils.

She slogged on. The bear had vanished. Gradually the muck beneath her feet grew firmer; she no longer had to fight for every step as the slime receded from her chest to her waist to her knees. Finally she was staggering behind Colin through a crowd of bulrushes to the hard grassy bank of safe ground. She sighed a long, tired, grateful sigh and stretched flat on the earth, wanting to stay as she was forever. Colin lay beside her, his breathing hoarse and choppy.

After a time she stirred and sat up. The sky to the east was pale, the fire noises faltering and far away. The Hairpin must have won. Colin turned his head and grinned at her. "Hate to say this, Julie, but you look like something that just crawled out of a swamp!"

She raised an eyebrow. "Well, I was out with this guy who wanted to take the scenic route ... " She stopped suddenly and grabbed his hand. "Colin, I *wouldn't* have crawled out if you hadn't been there. I—I was so darn scared my brain stalled. Sorry I was such a goof."

In the hazy half-dark she saw his face change. He

looked serious, almost grim. "So maybe we're even," he said. "I was stupid and scared too. Have been for a long time." He was silent a moment, then continued. "And you found me and climbed Darien and . . . " His hand tightened on hers. "C'mon, Champ, let's go home. I want to see my dad."

* * *

They walked into the snack bar and it exploded with a dozen voices, a dozen questions. Noise and people surrounded them. She saw the faces of Cecil Purdy, almost comical without the eyebrows, but with a great light in it; of her mother, the pinched lines around her mouth easing into a smile; of Aunt Mo, her expression curiously calm. She saw the smooth sleeping face of her little sister Katie, curled up in the porch swing by the far door. She saw Noah Clemens' face, the colour returned to it, his quiet eyes gazing at Colin in wondering recognition. And she saw the watchful, grave face of the police constable standing by the counter, at ease but alert.

Suddenly her legs gave way and she groped for a chair. She sat down heavily and closed her eyes. Her mother started to fuss then, bending to pull off the single wrecked running shoe, smoothing back the hair which hung in wet matted strands, rushing to get hot water and towels and soap, gently clicking her tongue and murmuring, "Oh, dear! Oh, Julie!"

as she sponged the blood and filth from her daughter's arms and the soot-streaked slime from her face.

Julie heard Noah speaking softly and opened her eyes. The three of them—Noah, Mr. Purdy and Colin—sat together at a table. Colin's face was white as he stared at Noah. How did I miss it? thought Julie. The same chin, the same hands, the same springy build, the same far look in the blue eyes.

Mr. Purdy held out the silver-framed picture. "This is your grandmother, son. My mother." His voice brightened. "And this fellow, whom I believe you've already met, is your great-uncle Noah." Colin went whiter still and his hands gripped the edge of the table. The policeman shifted his position slightly.

Noah took one of Colin's hands and held it. "Don't fret so, boy," he said. "Things'll work out in time. Your dad and I had a good long talk." He searched in his pocket, came up with something that gleamed silver in the light. "Almost forgot. Think this is properly yours." He dropped the carved signet ring into Colin's palm. "Gave it to your grandmother a long while ago. *C* for Clemens. Could just as easy stand for Colin though."

Julie saw tears in Colin's eyes and had to swallow quickly. I'm gonna bawl too if this keeps on, she thought. Then Noah began to chuckle quietly. "Say,

Colin, you know that hole behind the cabin your partner was poking around in? Nothin' much in there. Not yet anyway." He chuckled harder. "What it was, was a new pit. For my privy."

Colin started to grin. Mr. Purdy's shoulders shook. Then all three of them laughed and laughed, punching one another on the arm every now and then. Julie thought of the immaculate Paul Craven, with his spotless clothes and his perfect hands, mucking around in an outhouse and she laughed right along with them.

At last Noah leaned back, wiping his eyes. "Well now, Cecil. I've got a notion to buy some land hereabouts, settle down after all these years. You happen to know who owns that big parcel west of Big Rock Lake?" His gaze was bright and piercing.

Mr. Purdy looked a little strange, Julie thought. The smile of a moment earlier—which had made him seem less of a grump—suddenly disappeared, replaced by a guarded, watchful expression. "I believe that belongs to Mrs. Flanagan, Noah. Her late husband meant it for a hunting camp." He coughed, cleared his throat, then continued. "I—I hold the mortgage on all the Flanagan property at the moment."

"That so? Tell me, Cecil, what'd be a fair price these days?"

Mr. Purdy laughed nervously. "Probably more

than you can afford, Noah. City people have pushed values way up."

Noah laughed too. "Well now, Cecil, you didn't answer my question."

Mr. Purdy squirmed in his chair. "The current market rate's far too high. The land's full of rocks, you know. Why don't you wait a while?" The words were tumbling out of his mouth. "I'll find you some land later on. I'd be glad to advise you—"

Noah interrupted. "Would you say about five thousand altogether? Guess I could swing that." He stared at Cecil Purdy and a little smile played on his lips. "Probably be a help to Mrs. Flanagan right now too. Hear she's hard-pressed."

Mr. Purdy's red face turned a deeper red and he looked away. "I'm—I'm sure you'll have no trouble with the purchase." His voice sounded as if he were being strangled.

"Glad to hear it, Cecil. Don't like to see the wild taken over by city folk. First thing they do is build a shopping mall!" He chuckled and shook his head in disbelief.

Julie didn't know whether to laugh or cheer. She caught Colin's eye and winked gleefully. Guess Three Loons will be here for a while yet, she thought happily.

"Always had it in mind to set up a little sanctuary for the wild things," Noah was saying. He turned to Colin. "Need some help though. That interest you, young fellow?"

Julie watched the brightness flood into Colin's face. He glanced at his father. Cecil Purdy looked strange again, almost bewildered. Then he slumped back in his chair as if he'd just let go of something, and nodded at his son. "It's up to you, Colin."

The constable moved forward from the counter. "Can't give you any more time, Mr. Purdy. I'll have to take the boy to the station."

Colin stood up and turned swiftly to Noah. "Will —will you hold the job until—until I'm out of jail?"

The old man smiled gently. "I've waited forty years, son. I can wait a while longer."

Suddenly Colin was in front of her and she looked up. "Julie . . . thanks." He grinned his crazy grin. "It was quite a summer, huh, Champ?" He bent and kissed her on the cheek and then walked rapidly out the door, the policeman close behind. Julie's eyes blurred as she watched him go, and a phrase or two of his song drifted in her memory. " 'Cause the sun gonna shine in my back door some day . . . " She smiled. It might just come true.

Aunt Mo came in from the kitchen, switching off the overhead light on her way. Through the window, across Wandering Lake, Julie saw a pink sun pushing its way up from the calm skin of water like a blister. She yawned. It was tomorrow already. Or rather today. She yawned again. Time for bed.

Aunt Mo slid a piece of blueberry pie in front of her and all of a sudden she was ravenous. She dug in and put a huge forkful in her mouth. Oh-oh. Not too ladylike, she thought, glancing at her mother. Then she stopped chewing abruptly, puzzled at the look in her mother's eyes. She couldn't remember seeing it before. It was like—like wonder. Or admiration? Julie almost dropped her fork. Her mother admiring her? Ha! Here she was, her clothes a wreck, her shoes lost, her hair dirty and her feet filthy. She'd been out the whole night without permission, riding around on a mini-bike with a seventeen-year-old dropout who had just been arrested for robbery—and her mother was sitting there admiring her, for crying out loud!

Julie very nearly did cry, but grinned instead, remembering too late that her teeth were all purple. "Hey, Mom, this is great pie! You should try some. I baked it myself, you know."

"*You* baked a pie, Julie?

"Yep." She peered shyly at her mother. "It was sort of fun. Aunt Mo says I have a light touch with pastry." She speared three truant blueberries. "Uh, Mom, I was wondering—maybe you could show me how to cook some other stuff when we get home?" Maybe even chili sauce, she thought. What the heck, why not?

Her mother didn't answer. She was rummaging in the canvas travelling bag beside Katie. "Well, I don't know, Julie. Do you think you'll have time?" On the table she laid a navy-blue sweater, worn, old, but with two new leather patches neatly sewn on the elbows. "After all," she said softly, "you'll have to practise hard to win that trophy again." Her hand, warm, familiar, missed, closed over Julie's.

Julie's mouth fell open and for once no words came out. She couldn't think of anything to say. She remembered suddenly what Noah had said about a different drummer. Why, her mother had one too! Maybe everybody had one—Colin, and Mr. Purdy, and Noah, and Steve, and even Roxanna Peters. And me, of course, she said to herself. She smiled at her mother. If there were that many drummers around, no wonder she and her mom hadn't heard each other's music very well. You really have to listen hard, she thought sleepily, or else the parade gets messed up. And everybody, everybody in the whole world, is in the parade.